Douglas Stuart is an Emeritus Professor of International Relations at Dickinson College and a former Adjunct Research Professor at the U.S. Army War College. He is the author or editor of six books, four monographs and over thirty juried journal articles dealing with U.S. national security. Stuart is a former NATO Fellow and State Department Scholar Diplomat. He has been a visiting scholar at the Brookings Institution, the George Washington Elliott School, the International Institute for Strategic Studies (London) and the Australian National University. This is his first work of fiction.

Fair Game
A Holmes and Watson Adventure

Douglas Stuart

Fair Game
A Holmes and Watson Adventure

Vanguard Press

VANGUARD PAPERBACK

© Copyright 2023
Douglas Stuart

The right of Douglas Stuart to be identified as author of
this work has been asserted by him in accordance with the
Copyright, Designs and Patents Act 1988.

All Rights Reserved

No reproduction, copy or transmission of this publication
may be made without written permission.
No paragraph of this publication may be reproduced,
copied or transmitted save with the written permission of the
publisher, or in accordance with the provisions
of the Copyright Act 1956 (as amended).

Any person who commits any unauthorised act in relation to
this publication may be liable to criminal
prosecution and civil claims for damages.

A CIP catalogue record for this title is
available from the British Library.

ISBN 978-1-83794-013-4

This is a work of fiction. Names, characters, businesses, places, events and
incidents are either the product of the author's imagination or used in a
fictitious manner. Any resemblance to actual persons, living or dead, or actual
events is purely coincidental.

Vanguard Press is an imprint of
Pegasus Elliot Mackenzie Publishers Ltd.
www.pegasuspublishers.com

First Published in 2023

Vanguard Press
Sheraton House Castle Park
Cambridge England

Printed & Bound in Great Britain

Special thanks to Walter H. Loving III, for his support and guidance.

John H. Watson, MD
An account of my experiences with Sherlock Holmes
in the United States during the month of November 1904
To be opened by my estate on the
one hundredth anniversary of my death

Since I have no heirs, I assume that this document will be opened by some lawyer, banker or civil servant who has obtained the rights to the detritus of my life. I have chosen this date primarily as an act of whimsy, but also because the story cannot be told without references to secret government documents obtained through diplomatic — and other — means. Some may argue that I had an obligation to make these documents public as soon as I acquired them. Others will claim that the documents should never be released. A century after my death seems to be a reasonable compromise.

The story must also wait until both Sherlock Holmes and I are long dead, to avoid any possibility that we might be prosecuted for certain actions that we took during this case. For the record, I do not feel any special sense of guilt for my role in these events, and I have no reason to believe that Holmes regrets his actions, or their outcome.

I assume that the person reading this story is English, and that there is still an England in the twenty-first century. But I doubt that my nation will still hold its dominant place in the world. There are too many signs of decline and overreach at present. Nor do I hold out much hope that the Pax Britannica will have been replaced by Tennyson's 'parliament of man', capable of fostering world peace. While I applaud the goals of experiments like the Hague Convention I doubt that nations will take the necessary steps to convert their swords into ploughshares. Indeed, if the current British Government were to commit itself unconditionally to such an idealistic campaign I would oppose it as dangerously naive.

To the extent that world order is being imposed in the future I have come to share Holmes' view that it will be done by the United States. The trajectory of America's growth as a world power is truly breathtaking and its placement between two oceans gives it the luxury of choosing when and where to become involved in world affairs. As long as American leaders choose wisely, they should be able to continue that trajectory.

As this story illustrates, Washington is most likely to succeed in building its empire if it relies upon London for advice and support. As this story also illustrates, however, it will not be easy for my nation to accept a subordinate and supportive role in this evolving transatlantic relationship. I leave it to the reader to conclude whether Holmes and I deserve any blame or credit for moving Britain toward this reduced status.

One

"I have settled on the Panama, Watson."

I was quite familiar with my friend Sherlock Holmes' habit of breaking a long silence with some completely unexpected statement. It nonetheless took me several seconds before I realised that the topic was hats, rather than geography. The newly established nation of Panama was much in the news of late, and I had been following with interest the reports of American efforts to revive the failed project of the French Canal Company to link the Caribbean Sea and the Pacific Ocean. My first thoughts quite naturally went to these developments, until I looked up at Holmes, hovering over me with a straw hat in his hands.

Three days earlier Holmes had returned from Jermyn Street with two round boxes. The combination of an especially hot summer and the gradual retreat of his hairline had forced him to consider lightweight headgear. Prior to making his purchases Holmes had researched the topic with the same intellectual energy that had made him the world's most renowned consulting detective. After completing his preliminary research at the British Museum he engaged in extensive discussions with a sales agent at

Bates, and then purchased one Panama straw hat and one Tamsui hat from Japanese Formosa. Then he began his experiments.

The hats were soaked in water and dried, over and over again. They were subjected (for reasons that I could not fathom) to centrifuge and vacuum tests, followed by minute inspection with a magnifying lens. They were worn indoors and taken outside. Holmes also spent a good deal of time in front of the hall mirror, turning this way and that — behaviour that convinced me that my friend, who had recently turned fifty, was becoming vain.

But now Holmes had reached a decision. I resisted the temptation to ask him how he had come to prefer the Panama, but Holmes did not wait for my cue. "Allow me to describe the characteristics of this hat which I find so attractive. I should begin by noting that what is referred to as a Panama hat is actually produced in Ecuador. I concluded that this type of hat has several advantages over the Tamsui, including its ability to retain its shape in spite of rough treatment and dramatic changes in temperature and humidity…"

I rose to fill my sherry glass, and then settled in to hear more than I would ever care to know about straw.

After approximately twenty minutes my friend took note of my discomfort. "Watson, you appear to be in a particularly ill humour today. I hope that I am not boring you."

"I am afraid, Holmes, that I do not have your talent for concentrating on such mundane topics as cigar wrappers, thistles, and hats. I realise that this is your way of coping with the recent lack of challenging cases, but I was nonetheless beginning to lose patience with you. Please excuse my honesty."

"Honesty is to be relished, Watson, especially between old comrades in arms."

It had in fact been three months since we had confronted what Holmes would call a "problem worthy of my attention." That particular case had taken us to Holyroodhouse in Edinburgh, the official home of the Royal Family in Scotland. The case had several interesting elements, and it gave me the opportunity to return to one of my favourite cities. It also served as a useful distraction for me, since it occurred soon after my second wife passed away, and I was still grieving her loss. Some people may believe that physicians are immune to this type of depression since they see death on a regular basis. But the death of a loved one can be especially upsetting to a doctor precisely because he cannot help but wonder if he did enough to avoid or postpone this outcome. Was there a procedure that he might have overlooked? Was there a relevant article in a medical journal that he missed?

Two

Holmes and I were summoned to Edinburgh by Sir Lionel Canning, the curator of the Royal Collection, to assist in the recovery of a rare piece of jewellery called the Darnley Jewel, a heart-shaped locket of gold and enamel, festooned with rubies surrounding an Indian emerald. The locket had been stolen two days earlier.

We took an early morning train to Edinburgh, and arrived at our destination in mid-afternoon. Lord Canning met us at the station. As we travelled to Holyrood in his landau, he provided some background. "The Darnley locket is not only an extraordinary piece of jewellery, it is also an important part of our history. It was commissioned by Lady Margaret Douglas and became the property of her son, Henry Stuart, Lord Darnley who was the second husband of Queen Mary."

I reached back into my early education for the historical reference. "A brief, and by all accounts tumultuous, marriage that ended with Darnley's murder."

"Indeed, Doctor. His death had all the characteristics of one of your mysteries. Lord Darnley and Her Highness were only married for two years, and by most accounts the queen began to regret the union immediately after the wedding. They were living separately when Lord Darnley's residence was blown up in the middle of the night. Curiously, when they discovered his body it appeared that he had been strangled. No one was ever found guilty.

"There is also a degree of mystery surrounding the Darnley Jewel. It is assumed that Lord Darnley gave it to her highness as a gift at some point in their marriage. It is not clear what the queen did with it. Her Highness had a great affection for fine jewellery, which she accumulated for its own sake. But she also used many pieces as a form of currency, selling or gifting them to accomplish various policy goals. The Darnley Jewel may have been one of these instruments of royal diplomacy."

Canning then brought us back to the present. "The Darnley Jewel was purchased by Queen Victoria from a private dealer in 1843. It was sent to Holyrood by Her Royal Highness in 1901. Plans are in place for a major event to celebrate its addition to the Royal Collection. The king himself is scheduled to open the exhibit when he visits Edinburgh this summer. But before that event could take place the jewel was stolen in the middle of the night. What made this case unique were the circumstances of the theft. The robbery took place in front of three of our most reliable and experienced security guards. All three were too shocked by what they witnessed to take any action. That is why I decided to seek your help, Mr Holmes."

Looking out the windows of our carriage I realised that our driver was taking us down the Royal Mile. I recognised some of the small shops that were crammed together on both sides of the street, and I remembered how much I had enjoyed visiting these shops with my second wife on our honeymoon.

The road led down a gentle slope to a semi-circular drive. When we exited the carriage our eyes were immediately drawn to four identical towers, two on the northwest side of the building and two on the southwest side, which dominated the front of the palace.

Lord Canning pointed at the impressive edifice. "The original building was an Augustine Abbey, built in the twelfth century. It has been rebuilt many times since then."

Our host led us into the palace and took us directly to the famous Great Gallery. He chose not to speak, and allowed us to take our time in viewing the more than a hundred paintings of Scottish nobility, dating back to 330 BC. As we were leaving the hall Lord Canning said, "The palace has served as the home to numerous Scottish rulers. It is not an exaggeration to say that Holyrood is the hub of Scottish history." He paused for a moment and then said, "Just as the Darnley locket is a centrepiece of Scottish culture."

Our host then led us to a smaller room that housed several glass cases which contained impressive pieces of jewellery, small sculptures and vases. He pointed to a blank space between an ornate necklace and a collection of signet rings. "This is where the Darnley Jewel was supposed to be exhibited. I can never forgive myself if it is not recovered."

We followed our host down a narrow flight of stairs to the lower section of the palace, where we met with the three guards. Lord Canning showed us the room where the locket was kept while it was being prepared for the exhibition. Holmes stopped in front of the solid wooden door. He knelt down and extracted his magnifying lens. After a brief inspection of the lock he said, "No sign of forced entry. Would the door have been unlocked at the time of the theft?"

Sir Lionel looked at one of the guards, who said, "The door was locked and bolted. I checked it myself, earlier that night." He paused for a few seconds and then continued. "But it was wide open when the ghost walked through it."

Holmes went immediately on the offensive. "This is the first that I have heard mention of an apparition. On what grounds do you make this preposterous claim?"

All three were quick to reply:

"It was the ghost all right."

"It was the witch herself."

"It was Bald Agnes."

The most senior of the three explained. "She walked right past us, with the jewel in her hands. She was naked, with a greenish glow, no hair on her head, and moaning in a way that terrified us." He led us out into a long corridor and pointed. "She walked slowly to the end of this hall and then... just disappeared."

When he finished interviewing the guards Holmes informed them that we might need to speak with them again. Sir Lionel assured us that they would be at our disposal, and then he led us back to his office. "Holyroodhouse is well known for two things. First, it was Queen Mary's home after her return from France, and it was from here that she ruled over Scotland until she was overthrown. It is also famous for its ghost, who has been seen by many guests over the centuries." Canning explained that the apparition was Mrs Agnes Sampson, a widow and midwife who had the misfortune of being born in a time and place where people were obsessed with witchcraft. In 1591 she was accused of working with the devil to make King James VI infertile. As part of her interrogation her head was shaved and she was stripped and subjected to torture. She resisted this brutal treatment at first, but then ultimately succumbed, at which point she was taken to the gallows, where she was garrotted and her body was burned. Our host concluded his remarks by stating, "If ever there was a case for an unquiet spirit, it was this woman."

I said, "What a truly horrible account of human cruelty."

Holmes responded, "Indeed, Watson, but I reject out of hand any claim that our thief is a ghost. I will proceed on the assumption that we are dealing with a rather routine burglary and that the culprit is someone who is well known to you, Lord Canning."

Our host responded, "I am inclined to agree with you, Mr Holmes, that we are not dealing with the supernatural.

But why do you assume that the culprit is someone I know?"

"Because the thief had a key to the locked room, and I assume that you would only trust a very small number of individuals with this key."

"You are entirely correct, Mr Holmes. Very few people have access to the keys. I will check with all of these individuals to be sure that no one has lost a key, and then I will provide you with a list of names. I should think that there will be about fifteen…"

"We can narrow that list, Lord Canning, by focusing only on women."

Canning then summoned two members of the house staff, who led us to our spacious and well-appointed rooms on the second floor. Both rooms overlooked a beautifully maintained topiary. I took note of a lion resting next to a lamb, a griffin, and a unicorn.

Three

Our luggage had already been delivered to our rooms, so Holmes and I unpacked and then wasted no time in beginning our investigation, which took place in two stages. First, Holmes pursued the claim that the 'ghost' had vanished when she reached the end of the corridor. He requested comprehensive floor plans of the palace so that he could look for hidden passageways. This line of inquiry seemed to be fruitless at first, until Holmes discovered that the palace had undergone comprehensive reconstruction from 1671 to 1679. He requested a copy of the previous floor plan, from the late sixteenth century. When he superimposed this earlier plan on the current blueprint he was able to identify a space of approximately one meter which was hidden behind a cabinet at the end of the corridor. Neither Holmes nor I could squeeze through this space, but it would have been relatively easy for a small woman to pass through it, particularly if she was unencumbered by clothing.

We showed Lord Canning what we had discovered and he arranged for a small boy named Hamish to enter the passageway and trace it to its end. The boy was provided with a lantern, and a string was tied around his waist in case he lost his way. Holmes asked him to whistle as he made his way through the passage, to assure us that he was safe. "You're lucky that I am a good whistler," the boy said, and commenced to demonstrate his talent by whistling "Loch Lomond." Lord Canning placed his hand on the boy's shoulder and informed him that there was no need for him to whistle a tune. "You can just make a whistling sound so that we can keep track of you." The boy shrugged and disappeared into the hole. He began to whistle immediately.

I was not surprised that Canning had reacted immediately to the song, since it was popular among individuals who called for Scottish independence. Our host felt compelled to explain that Edinburgh was still a hotbed of opposition to British rule. "These Jacobites are so ungrateful. They enjoy the rights and benefits of membership in the greatest empire in world history, but they cultivate nostalgia for a Scottish history that is mostly myth. I sometimes wish we could give them the independence that they desire. They would be back begging for affiliation with Great Britain within a month."

When neither Holmes nor I responded to our host's diatribe we all turned our attention back to the soft sound of whistling coming from the narrow passageway. After several minutes there was a tug on the string and then the boy's voice: "I am out in the garden." We rushed outside and found the boy sitting next to the unicorn in the topiary. He showed us a wooden trap door covered with soil and grass that was completely hidden by the unicorn. Hamish pointed down: "It was hard to lift... lucky that I am strong." He flexed his biceps to convince us. We commended the young man for his courage, and Canning gave him some coins.

After the boy left we made a cursory tour of the garden but we were not surprised when we found no clues. Since the garden was not routinely guarded at night, the perpetrator had been free to escape in any direction once she exited the passageway.

After dinner with Canning our host escorted us back to the room where the jewel had been kept. At Holmes' request he had arranged for us to interview the two people who were responsible for preparing the Darnley locket for the upcoming exhibit.

Henry Cowley, a man of about fifty with a receding hairline and pince-nez, was the official jeweller of the Royal Collection. Canning had assured us that he was a master goldsmith, with decades of experience working with precious gems. Cowley informed us that he had been working on the Darnley Jewel for two months, cleaning it and preparing it for presentation. He introduced us to his assistant, a Miss Aileen McCauley. She was a relatively small young woman of striking good looks, with clear brown eyes and curly reddish hair. She explained that her job was to assist Mr Cowley in the preparation for the upcoming exhibit. "My most recent duty was to clean the gold chain that will accompany the locket in the exhibit." She informed us that she was the last person to see the jewel before the theft. "I am certain that I closed and locked the door before I left for the evening."

Holmes then asked Cowley and the young woman where they were on the night of the robbery. The jeweller replied, "We can vouch for each other. I invited Aileen to dinner at my house that evening. By the time that we were finished it had started to rain heavily, so I convinced her to stay the night."

Lord Canning added, "I can attest to this, Mr Holmes. When I sent a member of my staff to Henry's house to inform him of the robbery both he and Miss McCauley were there, and they came together to the palace."

"This is all very useful," said Holmes. "There remains only one more task for me at this time. With your indulgence, Miss McCauley, I will need to confirm that your hair is indeed your own, and not a wig. As you know, all three of the guards who were present during the robbery have stated that the so-called ghost was completely bald."

The young woman laughed, and leaned toward Holmes. "Have at it, sir."

My friend inspected Miss McCauley's hair and then tugged at it.

"Ouch. I did not expect you to be so… enthusiastic, Mr Holmes."

"My apologies, Miss McCauley. But I needed to be certain." Holmes asked a few more cursory questions of the two individuals, but it was clear to me that they were not going to be of help with our investigation. We thanked them and Canning dismissed them. When they were gone

Holmes said, "Watson, what is your opinion of Miss McCauley?"

"Well, she fits the physical description of the ghost — small and thin enough to take advantage of the narrow passageway. But Mr Cowley claims that she was with him on the night of the robbery, and more importantly, she could not have grown a full head of hair in the past few days…"

"Well done, Watson, a concise summary of the relevant facts." Then he directed his attention to Lord Canning. "Sir Lionel, have you completed your list of women who have access to the palace keys?"

"I completed it last night, Mr Holmes. There were only four names. But I composed the list before we discovered the secret passageway. I can state with certainly that Miss McCauley is the only one of the four with the physical characteristics needed to manoeuvre through that narrow space."

"Then we have a fascinating puzzle, gentlemen. Miss McCauley's hair and Mr Cowley's testimony balanced against the fact that she is the only woman with access to the Palace keys who is physically capable of committing the crime. We have much to consider, so I recommend that we retire to our rooms and reflect on this riddle."

I was not surprised when, soon after we had returned to our rooms, Holmes began to play his violin. I was pleased that he chose one of Mendelsohn's lieders, which made it easy for me to fall asleep.

The next day was focused on the second stage of our inquiry — the 'eerie green glow' that all three of the guards had reported. It was the thief's misfortune that she had played into my friend's impressive command of chemistry. Holmes immediately identified the source of the glow as phosphorescent body paint — "In all likelihood silver-activated zinc sulphide." Once we had this information it was easy to make inquiries at local chemists. On our third try the druggist confirmed that he did keep this compound in stock. "But I don't have any at the moment. Last week someone broke into my shop by the back door. I made a thorough inspection when I discovered the break in, and as far as I can ascertain the only thing that was taken was my silver-activated zinc sulphide. As you probably know, Mr Holmes, this is not a particularly expensive product. I have already placed an order to replace it. For the life of me, I can't think of why someone would go to the trouble of stealing it."

"Unless," said Holmes, "that person did not want to be identified as having purchased this product."

We thanked the chemist and left. On our walk back to Holyrood my friend stopped at a park bench and sat down. He placed his hands together in front of his mouth, and was silent for several minutes. I knew from past experience that I should leave him to his ruminations. When he finally spoke he said, "Watson, I need to give some thought to this case, before I return to the palace. You might take advantage of this time to revisit some of the locations that you remember from your honeymoon. I will meet you back at Holyroodhouse this afternoon."

I was tempted to protest, but in truth I was excited about Holmes' proposal. I flagged down a hansom and instructed the driver to take me to the Royal Botanical Gardens. It had been my wife's favourite sight in Edinburgh. When I entered I was offered a map, but I declined. I simply wanted to wander without any specific purpose. I was rewarded with several reminders of that day with my wife, her enthusiastic comments on this flower or that plant, and my nodding accommodation. She was never more alive than that day, in that place.

When I exited the gardens I hired another cab to take me across town to the recently opened North British Station Hotel. I had read about this addition to the nation's network of railway hotels and I decided that it was worth a visit. It was an imposing Victorian edifice complete with a clock tower. The article that I had read noted that the clocks in the tower were set two minutes ahead, to encourage guests not to miss their trains. I found a convenient wing chair in the corner of the lobby and enjoyed watching the comings and goings for some time. Then I decided to test the hotel's restaurant. The maître d' found me a small table at a window that overlooked the Edinburgh Castle, and then he provided a menu. He pointed to one item. "I recommend the salmon today, sir, and perhaps a glass of Sauvignon blanc to accompany it." I handed the menu back and said, "I am happy to defer to your expertise." The maître d' was so pleased that he actually bowed, and a few minutes later he rewarded me with an amuse-bouche of caviar in a light pastry.

I decided to walk back to the palace after the substantial meal. It gave me the opportunity to browse the small shops along the Royal Mile. I also stopped for coffee at a pub that my wife and I had visited during that unforgettable honeymoon.

When I arrived back at Holyroodhouse Holmes was waiting for me in the circular drive. "I hope that you enjoyed your walk through the Royal Gardens and your lunch at the railway hotel, Watson."

I was tempted to ask him if he had wasted his day following me, but instead I said, "All right, Holmes, explain how you could know my itinerary."

"Nothing could be simpler, Watson. You have spoken many times of the ideal afternoon that you spent with your wife in the gardens, and I remember that you read with great interest an article about the new North British Station Hotel here in Edinburgh."

I laughed and said, "If only the mystery of the missing locket was so... elementary."

"In that regard, Watson, my last few hours have proven to be very productive." Holmes directed me to a bench just outside of the palace entrance. Once we were settled in he said, "You will remember that Miss McCauley was the only woman with the physical characteristics required to accomplish the theft, but we had two pieces of information that appeared to exonerate her. The statements by her superior, Mr Cowley, could be discounted. The young woman could have slipped out of the house with an umbrella in the middle of the night while her host slept, or Cowley could be complicit in the theft. But the second, and seemingly unassailable, piece of evidence was that Miss McCauley had a full head of hair. I spent some time reflecting on this fact after we separated. Then it came to me that I had committed a very fundamental error. I had taken the statements of the three guards at face value, without considering that all three might have been incorrect about what they saw. Of course, I rejected out of hand their claims that the thief was the ghost of Bald Agnes, but I allowed myself to be misled by their other comments. I made this error in judgement because the guards were unanimous in their assertions and all three seemed to be sober and conscientious individuals who gave me no reason to suspect them of any involvement in the crime itself."

Holmes paused for several seconds and then continued. "You will remember, Watson, that early in our collaboration I explained my deductive method to you."

"I do indeed, Holmes. I believe you said that you examine the data, as an expert, and pronounce a specialist's opinion."[1]

"Quite so, and this is precisely what I failed to do with the information provided by the three guards. When I realised my error and revisited their witness statements, the next step in our investigation became clear."

---

[1] Holmes had made this statement in a particularly complicated case which I had titled The Sign of the Four.

I was not surprised by the intensity of my friend's self-criticism, since I knew from experience that he could be his own most caustic critic at times. When I asked him to explain the mistake that he had made he said, "I will explain as we go in search of Sir Lionel. There is no time to waste."

With the help of one of his assistants we found the curator of the Royal Collection in the Great Gallery, concentrating on a portrait. "It is Darnley himself, gentlemen. I should have introduced you to him the other day." The portrait depicted Darnley as a young military man, with a sword and metal chest protector. The artist had not been kind to his subject. He painted him looking to his left, with a notable sneer — not at all a likeable expression. Lord Canning said, "I was just thinking about placing this portrait above the locket when — if — we exhibit it."

Holmes interrupted our host: "Lord Canning, we need your assistance in gaining access to Miss McCauley's chambers."

Sir Lionel confirmed with one of his assistants that Miss McCauley was at work, and then led us upstairs. "I am happy to assist you, Mr Holmes, but I can assure you that we have already inspected her rooms for the locket."

"I am not surprised that you were unsuccessful, but there might still be some valuable evidence in her rooms, if we know what to look for." As we walked at a brisk pace to the young woman's chambers Holmes explained to our host: "We have wasted valuable time looking for a bald woman. We should have considered that the thief only appeared to be bald. Once I accepted this possibility my next step was clear. I visited four stores that specialised in women's clothing. I had no luck with the first three, but my persistence was rewarded at the fourth establishment."

My friend explained to Lord Canning what he discovered at this store: "A rubber swimming cap, Your Lordship. They have become very popular with women who wish to swim but keep their hair dry. I was fortunate to find a sales person who had recently sold a white swim cap to a young woman with auburn hair. She assured me that she would be able to recognise this person if that is necessary, but for now it was enough to justify this inspection of Miss McCauley's chambers. If we are fortunate we will find a white swimming cap that has been painted phosphorescent green."

"This is very interesting, Mr Holmes, but I am certain that if such an item was here my assistants would have brought it to my attention during their last search."

As Canning was speaking Holmes was inspecting some of the books and pamphlets on a shelf next to the bed. Then I noticed him looking carefully at a monogrammed handkerchief before putting it in his pocket. Holmes then turned his attention to the two waste bins in McCauley's quarters. He suddenly reached down and said, "Aha, it would appear that our young thief was smart enough to get rid of the damning swim cap, but she saw no need to do the same with these…" Holmes removed his hand from the waste bin and showed us a white rubber chin strap and two small circles of white rubber. "Our thief needed to cover her hair, but she had no need for the chin strap or for the pieces of the swim cap that covered her ears. I believe, Lord Canning, that our next step is obvious."

Lord Canning instructed his assistant to contact the three guards who had witnessed the robbery and tell them to meet us in the room where the theft took place. We met them in the hallway outside of Miss McCauley's workroom and entered without knocking.

Miss McCauley was alone, and I had the impression that she was not surprised to see us.

Holmes wasted no time. "Young lady, I am sure that you know why we are here. We are convinced that you are the 'bald ghost'."

"And how did you come to this conclusion, Mr Holmes?"

"Let me begin by citing two things which I found in your chambers which, while not conclusive, are at least reasons for suspicion. "First, I noticed that you had a collection of books relating to Scottish history as well as pamphlets in Gaelic calling for Scottish independence."

Miss McCauley replied, "If this was evidence of a crime you would have to arrest most of the people in Edinburgh."

"Indeed, but then there is this." Holmes reached into his jacket and removed the monogramed handkerchief. He pointed to the letters AS. "I asked myself why you would attempt to mislead people about your family name. The only explanation that I could come up with was that something about your family name might have caused suspicion, or at least raised unwelcome questions. I asked myself what could the letter S stand for that might be seen as controversial for a person employed at Holyroodhouse. The answer, of course, was Stuart, the family name of Lord Darnley. Can we assume that you are a direct descendent?"

After a moment's pause, she made no attempt to prevaricate. "You are correct, Mr Holmes, my family name is Stuart, not McCauley. I am a distant relative. But I chose to conceal this fact in order to obtain my job here at the palace. I was concerned that if I told Lord Canning, who is rabidly anti-Scot, that I was a descendent of the Stuarts he might not hire me." As she spoke she looked directly at Canning with an expression of intense dislike.

Holmes and I had seen some evidence of Lord Canning's prejudices regarding Scottish independence, so I was not surprised when my friend chose to change the subject.

"And then there is the much more dispositive evidence relating to the swim cap."

This comment had the expected impact. Miss McCauley — Miss Stuart — seemed to lose her confident and confrontational attitude. Now she was just a young woman who was hearing some very bad news.

Holmes pressed forward. "We spoke with the salesperson who sold you the swim cap. She is prepared to identify you in court. We also found these in your bedroom." Holmes displayed the two pieces of rubber that had covered the ears on the swim cap. Then he showed her the chin strap.

"Very well, Mr Holmes. I should have realised that the game was up when you were brought into the investigation. Let me begin by noting that I was not lying when I said that I felt compelled to change my name because of Lord Canning's bigotry. But this is not the only reason why I stole the locket. I took this action because I am a proud Scot. I could not countenance the Stuart locket, this important piece of Scottish history, being exhibited as part of the English Royal Collection. When the opportunity presented itself I became 'Bald Agnes' and simply walked away with the locket. Fortunately, all I needed to do was to play to the superstitions of our guards." She smiled as she said this, and nodded at the three guards, who were visibly discomfited.

Miss Stuart also explained that she had been walking in the garden one afternoon when she discovered the trap door under the unicorn. She equipped herself with a lantern and followed the narrow passageway until it arrived at the back of the cabinet, which she pushed open to discover the corridor that led to the room that held the jewel. "I doubt that I would have actually stolen the locket if I had not found the passageway. It was as if I was destined to act."

At this point, Holmes said, "I congratulate you, Miss Stuart, on this audacious scheme. But now that you have been found out, it is in your interest to tell us where you have hidden the Jewel. I am quite certain that any judge will be inclined to reduce your prison sentence if you return the stolen locket."

"I am sure that you are correct, Mr Holmes, but the Stuart Jewel is safely beyond your grasp, and it will remain so until Scotland has achieved its independence. At that time, the jewel will be the centrepiece of the Scottish Royal Collection."

Miss Stuart's prediction proved true. She confirmed that Henry Cowley shared her views on Scottish nationalism and that he had been involved in the plan to rob the locket from the outset. Soon after he had spoken with us and provided our thief with her alibi Cowley had set sail for France, along with the locket. When he arrived in Calais he boarded a train for southern France. From that point on, his whereabouts were completely unknown. Holmes sought the help of his brother Mycroft to extend the search, but the trail had gone cold.

In the end, The Case of the Bald Ghost proved to be quite easy to solve. But to this day the jewel has not been recovered. Holmes and I consoled ourselves with two days of relaxation in Edinburgh, including some casual shopping along the Royal Mile. I returned to Baker Street with a new cane, with a handle made from the antler of a red deer stag, native to the Highlands.

Four

Holmes pulled me back from my reflections. "I share your frustration with our current situation, Watson, but there is nothing to be done about it."

"You could reconsider the invitation to visit the United States. A change of scenery would do us both good, and President Roosevelt has accorded us a great honour by inviting us to join him on the reviewing stand when he visits Saint Louis in November. The fact that this will take place at the Saint Louis World's Fair makes it especially attractive. By all accounts it is an unprecedented event — a celebration not only of humanity's inventiveness but of its diversity as well. The press has described the fairgrounds as a 'city of ivory', with buildings of marble and glass surrounding a great clock made entirely of flowers. Exhibits from all over the world have been contributed, Holmes — replicas of the Grand Trianon, the Charlottenburg Castle, Japanese and Chinese palaces, and an entire compound recreating the jungles of the Philippine islands. One journalist counted ten thousand flags decorating the fairgrounds. At night the entire area — buildings, statues, and fountains — is electrically illuminated. The exposition also boasts the largest collection of automobiles in the world, as well as an aeronautical concourse pitting all manner of airships against each other. The sponsors of this competition are offering one hundred thousand dollars to anyone who can manoeuvre a flying machine through a prescribed slalom course at a speed of not less than fifteen miles per hour. The fair will also play host to the Olympic games…"

"You make it sound very exciting, Watson." Holmes paused for a moment and then picked up the argument. "But what would I do on the reviewing stand? I refuse to be paraded about as a curiosity."

"Celebrity, Holmes, it is quite a different thing."

"A dancing bear is a curiosity, Watson. If it can dance the tango it becomes a celebrity. The distinction is a small one, at best."

"I won't debate semantics with you, Holmes. I am tempted to take matters into my own hands by accepting the invitation on my behalf and communicating some polite excuse for your absence."

When Holmes did not respond I decided to allow a few more days to pass before raising the issue once again.

The next day I discovered that I had an unexpected ally in Holmes' brother Mycroft, who summoned us to meet him at his club. Holmes' brother was a founding member of the Diogenes Club, a unique institution which imposes strict prohibitions on social interaction. Any unauthorised conversation can result in a member's expulsion. This made it attractive only to men who were instinctively solitary and antisocial. It also made it an ideal venue for Mycroft to formulate and manage his highly sensitive policies in the service of the crown.

Mycroft greeted us in the Stranger's Room, the only place in the Diogenes Club where conversation was permitted. As was his habit, he wasted no time with welcoming remarks. "It has come to my attention, gentlemen, that you have been invited by the American president to be guests of honour at the Saint Louis World's Fair." He turned to Holmes and said, "I assume that you intend to turn down this invitation, Sherlock. I certainly would, under normal circumstances. But the present situation is not... normal.

"Whitehall is especially interested in working with Mr Roosevelt to oppose Russian domination of China and Korea. To this end we have been encouraging the Americans to enter into a defence pact with Japan. As you know, our government established its own alliance with Tokyo two years ago. If this alliance can be changed into a tripartite pact with the addition of the United States it would send a potent deterrent message not just to the Russians but also to their current allies, Germany and France."

My first thought was for the poor people of Korea, who were suffering under the indirect rule of Tokyo. But I chose to address the larger issue. "I admit, Mycroft, that I do not understand why our government entered into a mutual defence pact with Japan. It strikes me as a militaristic society that is committed to an aggressive and expansionist foreign policy."

"I share your concerns about Japan, Dr Watson, however Tokyo is the lesser of two evils at a time when Russia poses a more immediate threat to British interests in the Pacific region. But you have also put your finger on one of the reasons why we are anxious to encourage American support for either an official or unofficial tripartite alliance with ourselves and the Japanese. It will assist us not only to contain Moscow and its European allies but also to discourage Tokyo's instincts for regional dominance.

"It is my understanding that, as Mr Roosevelt's guests of honour, you both will have several occasions to be physically close to the president. This will give you gentlemen the opportunity to assist his bodyguards in insuring Mr Roosevelt's safety."

I asked if he had specific reasons to be concerned about Mr Roosevelt's safety.

"We have been very worried about threats to the American president since the assassination of his predecessor. You will remember that President McKinley's attacker was an anarchist — a Mr Czolgosz, who was executed soon after the attack. Our experts believe that he was one of a growing number of American anarchists who have become increasingly radicalised and prone to violence. This situation is made more dangerous by the ready availability of hand guns in the United States."

Mycroft paused and then concluded, "In confidence, I can also confirm that we are alert to the possibility that one of the governments that view Mr Roosevelt as an especially troublesome international actor may conclude that the problems that he can create outweigh the risks associated with his... termination. Russia is our most immediate concern, but it is not the only candidate."

Mycroft began to rise from his chair, signalling that our conversation was at an end. It was clear that he did not expect a decision from his brother at that time, and he did not receive one. Holmes remained silent as we exited the Diogenes Club and returned to Baker Street.

Two days later Holmes broached the topic of the invitation. "Watson, I admit that I am intrigued by your description of the events that will be taking place at the World's Fair. The aeronautical concourse is of particular interest to me. I wonder if the Wright brothers intend to compete in the aerial competition. Their flying machine has certain inherent advantages over other forms of aerial locomotion, but they will have to make extensive modifications in order to manoeuvre through a slalom course. There is also the matter of distance..."

At the time, I believed that it had been Mycroft's intervention that convinced Holmes to accept Mr Roosevelt's invitation. Three months would pass before I would discover the real reason for my friend's change of opinion on that afternoon.

Five

We scheduled our voyage so that we could make the crossing on the *RMS Lucania*, famous for both its speed and its luxurious accommodations. The ship was of such vast proportions and so well-constructed that the Atlantic squalls which were common at this time of year caused little inconvenience and no concern. The Cunard Company provided us with two adjoining suites, richly appointed in oak and mahogany, with velvet curtains covering the portholes. We were invited to dine at the captain's table on the first night of our voyage.

Our visit to the United States had been written up in the London dailies, and during our first two days on the ship we were occasionally subjected to idle and purposeless harassment by passengers — confirming Holmes' worst fears about the fate of 'curiosities'. By the morning of the third day, however, Holmes had established himself as an unprofitable target for conversation, not only by his curt and monosyllabic responses but also by his reliance upon members of the crew who spread a rumour that the great detective was actually on his way to a clinic in New York City that specialised in the treatment of rare and contagious diseases. His personal physician, Dr John Watson, encouraged people to maintain a safe distance…

Our trip was uneventful, aside from one minor distraction. On our third night at sea we found ourselves seated at dinner across from a dour individual in clerical garb who introduced himself as Reverend Richard Allen, of the Methodist denomination. I guessed his age at about fifty. My initial impression was of a man of average height, with receding brown hair and brown eyes, who had never smiled in his adult life. He made a great show of praying before our meal and then reading the bible sotto voce while he ate. He also made a point of criticizing those guests who elected to have wine with their meals. When pressed by another diner he informed us that he had just completed a three-year mission in Johannesburg and was on his way home to Philadelphia where he would be given his next posting.

The Reverend Allen had made such a bad impression at dinner that I was quite surprised when Holmes informed me at breakfast the next morning that he had requested that he and I be seated with the minister again that evening. I was even more surprised when, at the start of our dinner that evening, Holmes asked our companions if he might be permitted to quote his favourite prayer by John Wesley before our meal. In all my years with Holmes I had never known him to engage in public prayer. His request was met with an uncomfortable silence from the other guests and an approving nod from the cleric. With his head lowered, Holmes began,

> "Parent of Good, whose plenteous Grace
> O'er all thy Creatures flows,
> Humbly we ask thy Pow'r to bless
> The Food thy Love bestows."

The Reverend Allen was quick to commend my friend for his selection of such an appropriate, and inspiring, invocation. No one else, including myself, commented on this strange start to our dinner, and nothing else of note transpired during our meal.

Holmes spent much of the next few days in the ship's library, reading various articles by and about our host, President Roosevelt. After dinner on the night before our arrival in America he asked me to join him for "what promises to be an interesting experiment." Holmes explained what he intended to do and how I should play a role in his plan. I followed him down to a secluded section of the port side of the ship and I positioned myself behind a lifeboat. We waited in silence for about ten minutes, until the arrival of Reverend Allen.

"I must admit, Mr Holmes, that I do not understand why you asked me to join you here this evening."

"I thought that we needed to discuss some sensitive issues, Mr Allen, in a place where we cannot be overheard."

"And where, if I may ask, is your constant companion?'

"Watson does not know that we are meeting. He does not need to be implicated in this matter."

"This all sounds very suspicious, sir."

"Then it is best if I get right to the point. I am here this evening to give you the opportunity to purchase my complicity, for a fee of twenty thousand American dollars."

Allen laughed at this comment, and then stopped and stared at my friend. "I have no idea what you are talking about Holmes, but I see no reason for me to listen to another word." He turned on his heel and began to walk away. But he paused when Holmes said, "Don't you want to know what has led me to make such a proposal?"

He returned to face Holmes. "All right, what possible reason would I have for giving you such an enormous sum of money?"

"You have a stake in my silence. You cannot allow me to inform the authorities that you are not the Reverend Richard Allen. You are an imposter who is intent on gaining control of the Reverend Allen's substantial estate."

"And how did you come to the preposterous conclusion?"

"Two small incidents have combined to bring us here. The first occurred after our initial dinner together, when I took a stroll around the upper deck of the ship. As I came down the port side I saw you at the rail, enjoying a cigarette before retiring. I chose not to interrupt you, and I returned to my stateroom. The second small incident relates to the verse that I quoted prior to our second dinner.

"The first incident piqued my interest, because the founder of Methodism had opposed the use of tobacco, calling it a 'needless self-indulgence'. Since then the issue has been the subject of considerable debate among Methodist clergy, and it is no longer strange to see one of these individuals smoking. But you, my missionary friend, had made such an effort over dinner to impress us with your religiosity that I had difficulty imagining you as anything other than intensely conservative on such issues. This was just enough of an anomaly to justify a small experiment, in the form of the prayer prior to our dinner. I purposely chose a verse which I identified as having been written by John Wesley. In fact, it was a portion of a hymn composed by his brother, Charles. When you failed to correct me, I concluded that there was enough evidence to justify an inquiry into your credentials. I felt that we had to move quickly, however, before we arrived in New York and lost track of you. Fortunately, the *Lucania* is one of the first ships to be equipped with wireless telegraphy, so I was able to communicate with the Foreign and Commonwealth Office in London, whose very capable staff reached out to members of the Methodist community in Johannesburg with requests for information about the Reverend Richard Allen, including physical descriptions. I admit that I was disappointed when the first three responses arrived with very general descriptions — height, weight, hair colour — which were not significantly different from you. Of course, all this confirmed was that you might have chosen to replace this particular individual because of your similar physical characteristics.

"We also received a message from the local bishop, which spoke to the motive for an attempt to replace the real Reverend Allen. The bishop confirmed that the Reverend Allen had recently completed his three years of missionary service and that he was returning to his home. The bishop also noted that the Reverend Allen had informed him that he had been called back to Philadelphia in order to take over a considerable fortune following the death of the last member of his immediate family. Reverend Allen confided in the bishop that his grandfather had made a great deal of money by investing in railroads, and then his father had increased the family fortune by investments in real estate in the Philadelphia area. Reverend Allen advised the bishop that he intended to manage his family wealth so that he could leave it intact to the Methodist church on the occasion of his passing. This was enough to convince me that twenty thousand dollars was a quite reasonable sum to keep my silence."

By this time, our 'Reverend Allen' was red faced and sputtering with rage. "How dare you accuse me of stealing another man's identity? Will you also accuse me of having murdered this person? You have already admitted that I fit the physical descriptions that you have received from members of my flock. On what grounds, then, do you continue to harass me?"

"I mentioned that the first three telegraphs did indeed provide descriptions which might have exonerated you. This is not surprising since people are not usually very observant regarding physical characteristics, even of individuals whom they know quite well. Fortunately, we received another telegraph this morning which provided a very valuable, and I would say definitive, bit of information. This person gave a thorough physical description, including a statement that the Reverend Allen had attached earlobes, a relatively rare condition in which the bottom of the ear is connected directly to the sides of the head. You, sir, have the more common form of detached earlobes that hang free at the bottom. I have had occasion to discuss the difference between these two types of earlobes in a monograph on the underappreciated value of ears as a form of identification. This single bit of information is proof that you are not the Reverend Allen. Now, sir, all that we need to know is how you were able to acquire the identity of this person. Is this a case of murder, or did you simply take advantage of an opportunity when some incident led to the death of this individual?"

Our false missionary shrugged his shoulders and said, "For your information I did not harm the Reverend Allen. I merely fell to temptation when the occasion presented itself. I have been living in southern Africa for the past two years. I spent much of that time looking for gold, with no success. To make a bit of money I agreed to serve as the minister's guide on a mission trip to a particularly dangerous section of the Transvaal. The Reverend Allen wanted one more missionary experience before his return to America. He got more than he bargained for.

"As you know, it has been more than two years since the Boers surrendered. But the Afrikaner regions were still very dangerous for a British subject. Two days into our trek we were both fired upon. We never actually saw our attackers. After Allen was hit I tried to save him, but his wound was too severe, and there was no medical help to be had in that isolated region. I knew of Allen's plans for a return to the United States and of his inheritance, and so I decided to replace him."

At that point the imposter drew a small pistol from his coat pocket and aimed it at my friend. "I must admit, Mr Holmes, that I am disappointed that the world's greatest detective is a common blackmailer. You must realise that I cannot allow you to live. If I give in to your demand how can I be certain that you will not be back a month or a year later for another payment?"

"In my defence, mister… what shall I call you?"

"My name is Robert Henry."

"Well then, Mr Henry, in my defence, you might be surprised to learn that there is very little money in the consulting detective business. I do benefit financially from the stories that Watson writes, but of course I have to share my profits with the good doctor. Your contribution will help to insure my comfortable retirement."

The imposter waved his pistol at Holmes and instructed him to climb up on the railing.

'Retirement' was the word that Holmes and I had agreed upon as a trigger for action. As Holmes stepped toward the railing I slipped quietly from behind the lifeboat and brought the deer stag handle of my cane down on the wrist that was holding the gun. I was rewarded with a clear cracking sound as the pistol fell to the floor. Holmes stepped forward to seize the imposter but there was no need. He was sufficiently immobilised by the pain in his wrist.

"Well done, Watson. I am glad that it was not necessary for you to use your Webley in this case."

Over the next hour we turned our prisoner over to the captain, who instructed his security team to place Henry under guard. Holmes apologised to the captain for not informing him of his suspicions, explaining that he needed either more evidence or a confession before he could accuse the false missionary. "I needed to get him to talk, and I needed Watson as a witness to his words and actions." Holmes then led me to the telegraph office, where he transmitted a wireless message to the British Consulate in New York, with a request that they send a representative to the ship, with the authority to take Mr Henry into custody before he sets foot on American soil.

Over brandy that night I complimented Holmes on his handling of what I would later refer to as The Case of the False Cleric. "I do regret, however, that Mr Henry is likely to receive a fairly light sentence for his crimes."

"It is likely that he will be found guilty of fraud, Watson, and of threatening my life. He may also face some lesser charges relating to his failure to report the death of Reverend Allen. And it is at least possible that once the body of the Reverend Allen is discovered it will provide some evidence which leads to the prosecution of Mr Henry for murder. But the important point is that Mr Henry did not succeed in his criminal deception."

"True enough, Holmes, yet it seemed that you made it easy for him to confess to simply disposing of the body, when it was at least possible that he was actually guilty of killing Reverend Allen."

"You are correct, Watson. I provided Mr Henry with an alternative to an accusation of murder, for two reasons. First, because time was not on our side. We needed a confession of guilt before we reached port, so that the British authorities could take him into custody while he was still on British soil. I was concerned that if this matter was turned over to the American justice system it might never be brought to conclusion. My second and more important reason for helping our fictitious minister to confess to a lesser offense was that I was not at all confident that he would be found guilty if his case was to go to trial."

"I don't understand, Holmes. After you presented him with the proof that he was not who he claimed to be, he had no choice but to confess."

"That would have been true, if such proof had existed. In fact, my reference to attached and detached earlobes was a fiction, constructed by me on the spur-of-the-moment. We received no such statement from a witness in South Africa. I would say that we were fortunate that Mr Henry had never taken note of Reverend Allen's earlobes, but in fact it would have been rare indeed if he had been so observant."

Six

Our arrival in the Port of New York was dramatic. Neither Holmes nor I had visited the city previously. It is meant to be seen from its great harbour, preferably upwind. We stood at the bow rail and admired the Statue of Liberty. I had seen many photos of the monument, of course, and had also seen the quarter-scale replica in the Seine. I nonetheless had a catch in my throat when I viewed the actual statue. Its placement, alone on Bedloe's Island and visible from any location in the harbour, enhanced the emotional impact. I remembered that the actual name of the statue was 'Liberty Enlightening the World' — as much a statement of America's global ambitions as it was of the nation's tradition of welcoming 'the huddled masses'.

I was steeling myself for the tedium of debarkation when a member of the crew informed us that we were to be met by a representative of the American Government who would expedite our passport and customs inspections. Some minutes later, a young man who introduced himself as "Peter Hastings, a Foreign Service officer", appeared at our cabins. He was even taller and thinner than Holmes, all chin and Adam's apple. But his most distinctive personal characteristic was his curly red hair. I remember thinking that he would have been an excellent candidate for the 'Redheaded League', a fictitious organization that presented Holmes with one of his most interesting cases.

"It is a real pleasure to meet you, gentlemen. I don't mind telling you that this is the most interesting job that I have had since joining the State Department last year. I am scheduled to be posted to Italy in January and I am currently taking the department's four-month intensive language course…"

Hastings continued to chatter as he led us, accompanied by our porter, off the ship and up a flight of stairs to a small, glassed-in office which was identified on the door as the U.S. Customs Service. A small, bald man was facing us from the other side of a desk. Once inside the office Hastings immediately adopted a new persona. Like a young second lieutenant in the presence of a battle-hardened sergeant, Hastings attempted to establish his authority. He presented his credentials to the individual behind the desk and announced, "These gentlemen are guests of the United States Government. May I speak to the individual in charge to facilitate their arrival?"

The clerk advised him that the chief customs inspector was engaged in official duties at the other end of the pier.

"How soon will he be here?"

"Depends."

"On what?"

"On what he's doing over there."

Our Mr Hastings assured the clerk that this was unacceptable, and instructed him to fetch his superior immediately.

"I can't leave the office unattended."

"I am an agent of the United States Government, and fully capable of guarding your office in your absence."

"You're not an agent of the Customs Service, mister."

The ensuing argument showed signs of going on forever. Finally, Holmes intervened. "Might I suggest, gentlemen that Dr Watson and I remain here while you both go in search of the chief inspector?"

"That won't do, mister. You could walk right through that door and onto the street without clearing customs." The clerk indicated a door at the opposite side of the room from where we had entered.

A compromise was finally reached. Holmes and I, accompanied by our porter, were to remain in the office while the two civil servants went off to find the official in question. To ensure that we would not escape during his absence, the clerk locked the door that led out to the street and collected our passports. He then led Hastings out through the door by which we had entered, and with all the ceremony of the sealing of the pyramid of Cheops, locked it after himself. Within moments, they had disappeared into the huge and tumultuous pier.

We sat in the small office and watched through a large window as the passengers left the ship and were processed through the regular customs and immigration points at the front of the pier. My friend retained his composure at first, although I noticed that he was staring intently through the office window and becoming increasingly agitated. In due course Holmes began to pace rapidly, looking up and down the pier for the government functionaries. After nearly an hour he began to talk to himself, cursing quietly and waving his arms. I had only heard him use such language once before, under circumstances which provided much more justification.

I was even more astonished by what came next. Without a word of explanation, Holmes reached into his jacket and removed the small metal implement which he carried for cleaning and packing his pipe. He then proceeded to kneel in front of the door that opened onto the street and began to pick the lock!

"I say, Holmes, I don't think that's necessary. I'm sure that Hastings will be returning shortly with the customs people." But I might have been speaking to a deaf man for all the response that I received.

In a matter of seconds, the lock surrendered to my friend's practiced efforts, and Holmes was up and through the door, racing down the steps and out of sight. A few minutes later Hastings returned with the clerk and an individual whom I assumed to be the chief inspector. The clerk was the first to open the barrage. "Why is that door open? Where is the other man?"

Since I had no explanation to offer, I was struggling for something to say when Holmes rushed back into the office. He immediately went on the offensive. "Hastings, your inefficiency is unpardonable. You were gone for more than an hour while we were imprisoned in this room. Did you decide to take these gentlemen to lunch?"

The chief inspector entered the fray at this point. "Look here, mister, we can't have people wandering free in the streets without going through the proper procedures. Perhaps you think that you are above our laws, but I am here to tell you that you ain't. Why, for all I know you have already passed some contraband to someone."

"Please, Inspector," interjected the embarrassed and apologetic Hastings. "This is Mr Sherlock Holmes, the world-famous detective. He is an official guest of President Roosevelt… I am sorry Mr Holmes, I did not expect that we would have such difficulty locating the chief inspector. I had no idea how big this place is. We didn't, I mean, eat lunch…"

"Well," Holmes relented, "it is over now." Then he glowered at the two customs agents. "Unless these gentlemen wish to pursue the matter further?"

After an appropriately dramatic pause the man in charge of the pier decided that there was nothing to be gained by carrying the matter further. "Well, then, let's get on with it. But I will be filing a report on this incident and it will have all of your names on it. Now, Mr Famous Detective, are you transporting any foodstuffs or livestock into the United States?"

Seven

"I must say, Holmes, that I found your behaviour at the pier inexplicable." I had restrained myself for more than two hours, until the poor young man from the Department of State had deposited us at the front desk of the Algonquin Hotel, and with a last flurry of apologies, escaped. Before Holmes could respond to my comment we were interrupted by a woman's voice, calling my friend's name. I turned toward the voice and was startled to recognise a person who held a very special place in my, and especially my friend's, memory. It had been more than a decade since Holmes and I had seen this person, whom Holmes always referred to as "the woman." I remember writing at the conclusion of their last interaction — an account that I titled A Scandal in Bohemia — that "...the best plans of Mr Sherlock Holmes were beaten by a woman's wit." She was still the strikingly beautiful woman whom Holmes had described as having "a face that a man might die for." She was almost my height, with a natural elegance in her movement. She also had that same sparkle of intelligence in her eyes that has always set Holmes apart.

"Miss Irene Adler," I exclaimed. "What a nice surprise. I have followed your opera career with great interest. Am I correct that you are currently preparing for a role in the new Puccini opera?"

"I am Mrs Godfrey Norton now, Doctor. It is such a pleasure to see you again. And you as well, of course, Sherlock. And you are correct, Doctor, about my current plans. I will be premiering the role of Cio-Cio-San in *Madama Butterfly* at the Metropolitan Opera here in New York two seasons from now. In about three weeks I will also be performing some arias from that opera at the Met. It will be the first performance of these pieces in the United States."

Mrs Norton then surprised me by stating, "I can't tell you how grateful I am to both of you for coming to New York in time to help us with our very serious problem." She then turned to a man of about forty who was standing next to her. He was a few inches taller than his wife, with broad shoulders and the posture of an athlete. "Allow me to introduce you both to my husband, Godfrey."

I was reminded of the only time that I had seen Mr Norton. It was at a distance, and on that occasion I had described him as "a remarkably handsome man, dark, aquiline and moustached." In the intervening years, he had lost the facial hair, and acquired some grey above his ears.

Norton shook my hand, and impressed me with the strength of his grip. "It is my pleasure to meet you in person, Doctor… and to see you again, Mr Holmes. We last met at my wedding to Irene at the Church of Saint Monica." Holmes smiled at this comment. "It was indeed our first and last meeting, Mr Norton. I remember serving as a witness to the ceremony, although I did so disguised as a rather dishevelled groom."

"Quite so, Mr Holmes. You provided indispensable assistance to my wife and me on that occasion, and I sincerely hope that you can do so again, when we are so in need of your unique skills."

Mrs Norton took up the discussion at this point. "As I mentioned in the letter that I sent you in August, Sherlock, my husband has been charged with the theft of a large quantity of bearer bonds. He is entirely innocent, but the evidence against him appears to be quite strong. Our lawyer was able to obtain a postponement of the trial until mid-November — three days from now — so that you would have an opportunity to prove his innocence. You and Dr Watson are truly our last resort."

'The woman' then put her hand on Sherlock's arm and said, "I am so grateful that you are here. I went to the docks this morning to meet you as you disembarked, and I was so concerned when I was not able to find you."

With these few words Mrs Norton solved four small mysteries for me. What had really changed Holmes's mind about coming to America? Why had he insisted on coming nearly two weeks before we were expected to attend the festivities at the World's Fair? Why had he proposed that we spend our first days in New York City before traveling to Saint Louis? And finally, what had caused Holmes to be so agitated, and behave so erratically, at the pier? It was now clear to me that he had seen Mrs Norton from the window in our small customs office, but that she had gone by the time that Holmes escaped from our confinement and ran down the stairs.

"Mrs Norton, we are at your service. Watson and I will use what little time is available to us to solve this case and vindicate your husband. We only have two days before the trial, but we have a significant advantage — we can be absolutely certain that Mr Norton is innocent."

"Thank you so much, Sherlock. As I mentioned in my letter, President Roosevelt is a personal friend, and while I could not ask him to intervene directly on my husband's behalf, he was kind enough to offer the resources of the New York City Police to assist you in your investigation. I have taken the liberty of arranging for you to meet with a Detective Inspector named Meyer Abrams at police headquarters at nine tomorrow morning."

"I will be there, Mrs Norton. Watson?"

"By all means, Holmes."

Eight

The next morning the weather was brisk, but we had come prepared, with mackintoshes, scarves and gloves. Holmes's straw hat had served its purpose during the summer and was now retired to the coat closet at 221B Baker Street. He was back to wearing his deerstalker, which provided coverage for his ears, as needed. I chose not to bring headgear, and opted instead to use a scarf to cover my ears.

We had arranged to meet Inspector Abrams at police headquarters, located at 300 Mulberry Street in a particularly unsavoury part of the city. We wasted no time getting from our hansom to the entrance of our destination. But we were not prepared for the chaos that greeted us inside. The reception area was full of policemen, victims of crimes, and criminals, all shouting over each other. Two very large men were a few feet away from us, surrounded by three police officers. Both men were shackled, with their manacles in front of them, but this did not prohibit them from carrying on with the argument that I assume had led to their arrest. As we stood there one of the two attempted to throttle the other. The three officers attempted to restrain him but he continued to strangle his enemy. At this moment a small man with the physical appearance of a lightweight boxer moved through the crowd, and in one smooth motion removed his billy club from his belt and brought it across the right knee of the prisoner. He collapsed immediately and the three officers pounced on him. The small man twirled his truncheon with practiced ease and stepped toward us.

"Mr Holmes and Doctor Watson, I believe. I am, of course, familiar with some of your exploits, Mr Holmes, as they have been so dramatically recounted by Dr Watson. But I admit that the main reason why I agreed to assist you is because the request came from President Roosevelt, whom I hold in such high regard. He was the best police commissioner this city has ever had. On a personal note I can report that he was wise enough to recognise that the police would never be able to do their job in the Lower East Side unless some officers spoke Yiddish. I am a beneficiary of this insight."

Abrams moved on the balls of his feet and seemed to be constantly on the alert. He was of middle age, balding, with a welcoming smile. I noticed that he immediately made eye contact, and it struck me that he would be a particularly effective interrogator.

Holmes and I both shook his hand and then my friend said, "I am very grateful to you, Inspector, and to President Roosevelt, for your offer of assistance. Would it be possible for us to visit the crime scene as a first step in our inquiry?"

Abrams led us outside, where he had a landau waiting. Once we were settled in, he provided both of us with maps of the city. "With the compliments of the New York Police Department." I opened my map and he placed a finger on our location.

"From here it is a short walk to the infamous Five Points district of Manhattan, which used to have the reputation as the most dangerous neighbourhood in the world. We are also close to other poor neighbourhoods — the Bowery, Chinatown and Little Italy — each with its own complex identity and its own rules of behaviour."

As our carriage crept forward Abrams pointed out a church which was not far from police headquarters. "If you are looking for the epicentre of the violent history of New York, you can't do better than the Basilica of Saint Patrick's. During much of the nineteenth century it was the site of almost constant struggle, serving as a fortress for Irish and Italian Catholics threatened by competing ethnic and religious groups as well as anti-immigrant gangs. You see the brick wall attached to the church. It surrounds a small cemetery, but if you look closely you will see the holes in the brickwork, where defenders of the church mounted their rifles. The church has played a key role in the gradual acquisition of political influence by both law abiding and corrupt settlers."

Abrams continued: "In recent years, the Chinese have presented us with the biggest problems. There are about seven thousand living in the Chinatown area. Many of them were chased out of California over the past couple of decades. They are plagued by especially violent gangs, called Tongs. When they are not killing each other, they are terrorizing the locals. The police have great difficulty coping with these criminals, since we have only a handful of Chinese speaking officers who understand their culture. I do like their restaurants, however..."

Abrams continued to discuss the history of his city as we moved north. "New York has grown to over three million residents, fuelled by a constant stream of immigrants, most of whom have come from Eastern and Southern Europe in recent years. The challenge that we face is to adapt to this flood, without being overwhelmed by it. Much of the credit for our success must be given to Mr Roosevelt's reforms as police commissioner. Ah, I see that we are about to arrive at our destination."

The contrast with Mulberry Street could not have been more stark. Godfrey Norton was a junior partner in a law firm that occupied a prestigious address overlooking Central Park. We were greeted by one of the three senior partners, a Mr Harding. Impeccably dressed in a black three-piece suit with blue pinstripes and a dark red silk tie, Harding exuded confidence and authority. I could imagine him in full command of a jury. "Thank you for coming, gentlemen. This is a terrible problem for our firm. I would never have suspected Godfrey of taking such an action. I was the one who reported the theft to the police."

Holmes wasted no time. "Would it be possible for us to look at the office where the theft took place?"

Abrams interjected that the room had been padlocked by the police to insure that no one tampered with it prior to the trial. "I have the key, however, and will be happy to give you gentlemen access to the room, under my supervision."

Harding led us to a door on the second floor and indicated the padlock. "No one has been allowed in this room since the crime was reported. This has created some inconvenience for us, but we understand why such precautions were necessary."

Abrams unlocked the door and we entered a large room that was clearly designed for both business meetings and social occasions. One half of the room was built around a table that seated six, positioned in front of a bow window that overlooked the park. The other half of the room was dominated by an ornate desk, positioned directly under a massive chandelier.

"The desk is the most interesting thing in this room," noted our host. "It is Austrian, a Biedermeier roll top. As you can see, the chandelier matches the desk, with the same rose decorations and the same type of wood. I purchased both pieces on behalf of the firm during one of my trips to Europe."

Harding pointed to an open wall safe directly opposite the door through which we had entered. "This is where we were holding a large quantity of bearer bonds for a client, in preparation for a real estate purchase. Only the senior and junior partners know the combination. Whenever we use the safe we position a clerk at the desk just outside of this room, as an additional security measure. I placed the bonds in the safe myself, on Tuesday morning, August the 12th. I then left the room and the clerk locked the door. Only one person entered and left the room after me that day, Godfrey Norton. So when it was discovered that the bonds had been stolen, the police wasted no time in questioning, and then arresting, Mr Norton. As you know, gentlemen, Godfrey claims to be innocent, and we were unable to find the bonds. But since he had gone out for lunch that day after entering this room, he could have concealed them anywhere while he was out of the building."

Holmes crossed the room and inspected the safe. Then he walked over to the other half of the room. "Thank you for this very concise summary of events, Mr Harding." With that, Holmes sat down in an overstuffed chair and began to fill his pipe. He sat in silence for some time, smoking and surveying the room. Then he spoke to no one in particular. "Four possibilities present themselves. Either Mr Norton is guilty and he removed the bonds from this building, or Mr Norton is guilty and the bonds are hidden in this room, or you, Mr Hastings, are guilty and the bonds are hidden in this room, or you, Mr Hastings, absconded with the bonds when you left this room." Before Hastings could speak, Holmes continued, "If either the second or third possibility is correct, then this interesting desk is the most likely hiding place." He pointed toward the Biedermeier roll top. "Would it be possible, Detective Abrams, for the police to call upon some experts to make a close and thorough inspection of this desk? And I would hope that such an inspection could take place before Mr Norton's trial begins in two days."

"I will be happy to recruit such experts, Mr Homes. In fact, we have used a firm that specialises in antique furniture in the past, and I should be able to arrange for them to visit this office tomorrow morning."

"Excellent. Then I see no more need for our continued presence here today."

With that, our party vacated the room and Abrams once again engaged the padlock. After we exited the building Holmes thanked the inspector and asked if he might meet him back at police headquarters later that afternoon. Abrams agreed and departed in the landau. "Watson, I think we can reward ourselves with a stroll through the park."

Central Park proved to be a welcome escape from the noise and soot that plagued most New York streets. Referring to the map that Abrams had provided, we followed a path that led us into the park and to the Bethesda Fountain. We were impressed by its size, and by the statue of the Angel of the Waters in its centre. I remembered something that I had read in preparation for our trip. "The Angel is a celebration of a successful engineering feat, Holmes, the completion of the Croton Aqueduct in 1842, which brings fresh water to New York from Westchester County — a distance of more than forty miles."

"You never cease to amaze me, Watson, with your capacity to record and recount minutiae."

I could tell that my friend was being sarcastic, so I ended my monologue and focused on the scenery. After a pleasant walk we exited the Park on the West side and hailed a hansom, which took us to a restaurant located near our hotel.

The concierge at the Algonquin had recommended Delmonico's to us, and we were not disappointed. After oysters and champagne we both ordered their special, the Delmonico steak, with sautéed spinach and a nice claret. Our waiter recommended that we order the steak 'black and red' — charred on the outside and medium rare on the inside. This proved to be good advice. After our meal Holmes informed me that it was time for him to meet with Inspector Abrams at police headquarters. He encouraged me to return to our hotel and catch up on some much-needed rest. We hailed another cab, which deposited me at the Algonquin and then continued on with my friend to his destination. The heavy meal and my travel weariness combined to insure that I was asleep soon after returning to my room.

Nine

It was well after midnight when I was awakened by a knock on my door. Holmes was in high spirits, clapping his hands together and pacing in my room. "It has been a most eventful evening, Watson. You will remember that I had an appointment with Inspector Abrams after you and I separated. My reason for meeting him was to enlist him in a small venture. He agreed to return with me to the law office and to bring along one additional officer. We arrived at our location in late afternoon and positioned ourselves across the street until the occupants of the building left for the day. We took particular note of Harding's departure, and soon after we crossed the street and knocked on the door. When, as we hoped, there was no answer, Abrams used a key that he had obtained from the law firm and led us up to the second floor. He opened the padlock and then gave both keys to his assistant, with instructions to lock us in and then position himself across the street at a spot from which he could see the bow window. We settled in to await developments. Our patience was rewarded at about eleven o'clock, when we heard a cracking sound indicating an assault on the padlock. Abrams and I moved swiftly to our positions behind the curtains that bracketed the bow window, and I was not surprised to see our Mr Harding enter the room with a crowbar. He walked directly to the wall on the right side of desk. He removed a landscape painting and exposed a small lever built into the wall. He pulled down on the lever, activating a motor which lowered the large chandelier from the ceiling until it hovered just a few inches above the desk. Harding then proceeded to lower four chains attached to the chandelier. Each chain had a hook on the end. He attached these hooks to four decorative roses which protruded from the front, back and sides of the desk. He then returned to the lever and lifted it up, activating the motor once again and raising the chandelier, along with the entire top half of the desk, above his head. We were not surprised to see him reach into the exposed bottom half of the desk and come up with what we knew would be the bearer bonds. It was a classic instance of catching the thief red-handed.

"Abrams and I stepped out from behind the curtains and Harding gasped. The inspector went to the bow window and signalled for his subordinate to join us. Abrams pointed to the lever and said, 'I assume that you are the only member of the firm that knew about the hidden compartment and the mechanism in the wall?'

"Harding recognised immediately that he had no realistic defence, so he saw no reason not to explain his actions. Without any encouragement from us, he stated that he had the electric motor installed some years ago, while his two partners were on vacation.

"'I was forced into this crime by my partners. When our firm was founded the three partners entered into an agreement that any two senior members could vote to remove the third member, with a modest financial compensation. I recently discovered that they were preparing to take such action against me, for reasons that do not have to be explained here. I was confronted with the prospect of unemployment, with a pension that would not cover my expenses. The bearer bonds were my insurance against such an eventuality. I do regret that my actions led to Norton's arrest.'"

"'But,' Abrams observed, 'you were willing to see him found guilty and imprisoned.'

"The other officer arrived and within minutes Harding was manacled, marched out of the building, and placed in the police wagon. Abrams instructed his driver to return me to this hotel on the way downtown. Now, Watson, I will attempt to get some sleep. I am sure that Mr and Mrs Norton will be anxious to hear about these developments tomorrow."

Not surprisingly, the couple was overjoyed — overwhelmed — when Holmes gave them the news the next day in the lobby of the Algonquin. Norton expressed his sincere thanks, and then said, "I never would have suspected Harding of this. He was always friendly and supportive." Irene pressed Holmes for some details. "What led you to suspect that the bonds were hidden in the desk, Sherlock?"

"It was not the desk that piqued my interest. It was the chandelier which was placed directly above it. I was struck by the size of the links in the chain which connected it to the ceiling. There was no obvious reason for such a substantial chain, unless it was designed to hold some great weight."

After some additional pleasant conversation and a promise by Holmes that he would be present at Mr Norton's trial the next day in case his testimony was required, our guests rose to depart. As they started for the exit, however, Norton's wife told her husband that he should engage a cab and that she would be along shortly. After Norton had departed, Irene Adler Norton smiled at us. "It is a nice coincidence, Sherlock, that you used the same ploy to catch Harding that you employed to trick me into disclosing the location of the photograph."

"Not exactly the same ploy, Mrs Norton. In your case I started a fire that threatened to destroy everything in your study. You reacted as I expected, and ran to save the photograph, which had been hidden behind a sliding panel in the wall. In Harding's case, I simply threatened him with an imminent close inspection of his desk."

"I am pleased to report that that photo remains hidden to this day, and that it has never been necessary for me to make it public. I should also mention that it is not necessary to prance around this issue in Godfrey's presence. He has known about the situation since the day he asked me to marry him. I told him all about what you, Doctor Watson, have called the Scandal in Bohemia at that moment, and I even offered to show him the photograph. He assured me that this was not necessary, and he said that all that mattered was that I was willing to marry him. He only asked one question: Did I still love the man who was in the photo with me? I assured him that I no longer even liked this person. I was not surprised by Godfrey's reaction, but men can be unpredictable regarding such matters. I was quite prepared to walk away from him if he had behaved in a jealous or possessive manner.

"I had to ask Godfrey to make another difficult decision one day after our wedding. That is when I told him that we needed to leave London immediately, without informing his friends or relatives. When he asked for an explanation I told him that the world-famous detective, Sherlock Holmes, had been employed to retrieve the photo, and it was only a matter of time before he succeeded. I explained how you tricked me into disclosing the location of the photo, Mr Holmes, and I knew that you would soon be at my front door. Godfrey understood, and we caught the five fifteen train to Southampton the next morning."

Then Mrs Norton surprised me by her next comment.

"I will always be grateful to you, Sherlock, for tracking me down soon after our arrival in France, with your message that you had received assurances from the man in the photo that he would no longer seek to obtain it, as long as I agreed to keep it hidden. This made it possible for me to continue my opera career and for Godfrey and me to return to London from time to time."

I intervened at this point to assure Mrs Norton that we were pleased that we could be of help on this occasion, and that we were also pleased that the photograph which had been at the centre of the scandal was still a well-guarded secret.

Irene shook our hands and prepared to leave. "I look forward to seeing both of you at the welcoming event at the White House next week." With that, 'the woman' was gone, and Holmes and I were left to fend for ourselves.

Ten

Since we had three days to ourselves, Holmes and I agreed to pursue our separate interests and then reconnect prior to our scheduled trip to Washington. Holmes chose to stay in New York, where, as promised, he attended Godfrey Norton's very brief trial. He would later inform me that there was no need for him to testify, since Abrams provided the court with a thorough account of what had transpired at the law firm. When he was finished the judge made a point of singling my friend out and thanking him from the bench for the role that he had played in serving the cause of justice.

Holmes spent the rest of that day at the American Museum of Natural History where he was treated like royalty by the director of the Halls of Gems and Minerals. His private tour included ample time with the Star of India, a stunning blue sapphire which Holmes had liberated from a particularly dangerous group of jewel thieves some years earlier.

On his next day in New York, Holmes took advantage of his free time to tour the massive excavation project which would soon provide New Yorkers with a comprehensive subway system. The first portion of the system, the Manhattan Main Line, had opened just one week prior to our arrival in New York, and Holmes was among its first riders. His guide took him to the City Hall station, meant to be the jewel in the crown of the system, with a domed entrance, stained glass skylights and brass chandeliers. Holmes reported that "London's underground system is of course more extensive, having a four decade head start on the Americans. But I was nonetheless impressed with both their progress to date and their plans for the future."

For my part, I chose to take advantage of my presence on the East Coast of the United States to visit the Gettysburg Battlefield. I had a great interest in this military turning point in the American Civil War, and I was anxious to see it in person. I took an early morning train to the town of Gettysburg, checked into a modest hotel near the battlefield, and then hired a very competent guide. On his advice we toured the battlefield on horseback. Over a full afternoon the guide showed me many of the most well-known locations, including Culp's Hill, Cemetery Ridge and Little Round Top. At each location my guide, a retired army officer, gave me the option of viewing it from the point of view of a general, a mid-level officer, a sergeant or a simple front-line recruit. He also allowed me to choose between the Confederate and the Union perspective. He was such a skilled storyteller that at times I could smell the gunpowder and hear the cries of wounded men.

My guide ended our tour at the place where the president had presented his famous Gettysburg Address.

He collected my horse, presented me with a pamphlet that included the famous address, and said goodbye, leaving me to spend some time alone. As I read the words I was reminded that the war still had to be won at the time that Lincoln gave this speech. But the president also understood that after victory was achieved he and his nation would face the challenge of North-South reconciliation. Reading his words convinced me that if his life had not been cut short he would have succeeded in this double mission. Instead, the burden fell on his Vice President, who was not up to the task.

These thoughts stayed with me during my dinner that evening, and late into the night. The next morning, on the advice of my guide I took a local train to the nearby town of Carlisle and found a convenient hotel in the centre of town. Carlisle had been one of the western outposts of pre-revolutionary America, and a frontier town that was frequently threatened by Indian tribes. I was informed by my guide in Gettysburg that Carlisle was also where President George Washington reviewed the troops who were sent to Pennsylvania to suppress the Whiskey Rebellion. The cause of the revolt was local resistance to government taxation of whiskey producers. I resisted the temptation to ask my guide why this was any different than British attempts to force the citizens of Boston to pay a tax on tea.

I had a pleasant lunch near the town jail, which had been modelled after a fortress that I had previously visited in the town of Carlisle in northwest England. Then I hired a carriage to take me the short distance to the Carlisle Indian Industrial School. Under the leadership of Brigadier General Richard Henry Pratt, the school had hosted hundreds of American Indians, with the goal of transforming them into productive and responsible citizens. Pratt had just stepped down from his post as superintendent at the time of my visit, but his goals were still celebrated by my two tour guides, both of whom quoted Pratt's motto: "Kill the Indian, save the man."

As one of the guides explained: "The general believes that the red man and the white man are 'equals' and that with the right education Indians can become valued members of our society."

I was impressed by this argument, and reminded of similar claims by British scholars and policy makers regarding 'our Indians.' During my time with the Fifth Northumberland Fusiliers, I had witnessed similar efforts by British educators to introduce Indian youth to the principles that undergirded British democracy. In their own way, these idealistic teachers contributed as much as any infantry officer to the expansion and preservation of Britain's Empire.

My guides took me to one of the dormitories (simple, clean and orderly) where I was introduced to three of the students. They were all about fifteen years of age, with varying degrees of English language proficiency. All three had Christian first names. One of the guides asked them what sports teams they were on. They all replied that they played football.

"When I was your age" I said, "my favourite game was rugby." They all looked at me with confusion, so I let the discussion drop. They seemed to be relieved when my guides led me away.

The high point of my tour was when I was allowed to look in on one of the classes at the School. The students were memorizing a portion of Longfellow's epic poem — "The Song of Hiawatha." The excerpt involved a call to the leaders of various Indian tribes to end their 'quarrels... wars and bloodshed.' The teacher was using a long pointer to help the students follow the words on the blackboard, and the students seemed to be admirably attentive.

At the end of my tour I returned to my hotel for an early dinner and a long night's sleep. I took an early train from Carlisle to New York the next morning so that I was back at the Algonquin by sunset.

Young Hastings met us at our hotel the next morning and accompanied us on the train to Washington. The train was not particularly comfortable or fast. We were also disappointed when we arrived at the Baltimore and Potomac Station in Washington. Hastings felt the need to apologise to us for the dingy surroundings. "If you gentlemen come back to Washington in a couple of years you will be able to visit our new Union Station, which will be one of the world's most impressive buildings. The city will also be greatly improved by the construction of the Station, which will require us to completely level the Swampoodle district — a disreputable and dangerous neighbourhood."

Hastings had arranged for rooms at the recently remodelled Willard Hotel, an impressive Beaux-Arts structure that was very popular with politicians and those seeking to influence politicians. Hastings pointed to a secluded corner of the lobby. "President Grant used to hide from influence peddlers over there. He invented the term lobbyist to describe these annoying individuals." After checking us into the hotel, Hastings said that he would be back to escort us to the presidential reception that evening, and then he bid us farewell.

The Willard was a centrally located establishment — walking distance from the White House. It was also close to the Smithsonian Museum complex, the product of a bequest from James Smithson, a British chemist and mineralogist who had never visited the United States. Since we still had several hours before the evening festivities we took advantage of this proximity to visit the Smithsonian Museum of Arts and Industry. The collection was very diverse and comprehensive — including musical instruments, ship models, and a massive cast of a whale which was suspended from the ceiling. We regretted that we had to return to our hotel after only three hours at the Museum.

Eleven

We arrived at the reception shortly after seven. The purpose of the event was to welcome the international guests who would be traveling the next day to Saint Louis to join Mr Roosevelt as guests of honour when he gives a speech at the World's Fair. Tables were distributed in a semi-circle in front of a large fountain on the north lawn, facing the North Portico of the White House. Holmes found a table that was on the side. I assumed that this was motivated by his desire not to be conspicuous, but in truth he and I were minor members of a guest list that included royalty from three nations, five elected heads of state, two scientists, and the conductor of the Berlin Philharmonic. Holmes' arrival was nonetheless greeted with considerable attention and even a ripple of applause. My friend was more than a little discomfited by this attention, and when I mentioned that we had rarely been greeted so enthusiastically Holmes nodded, without much interest.

His mood picked up immediately, however, when we were joined at our table by Mr and Mrs Godfrey Norton. Irene informed us that she would be performing for us this evening "one of the arias that I will be singing in about two weeks at the Met." It struck me that although I had followed her career with great interest, this would be the first time that I would actually hear her sing.

By the time that we arrived the orchestra had already begun to perform for the guests. I recognised some familiar opera pieces and some popular waltzes. Mrs Norton explained that they were the Philippine Constabulary Band, which was brought to the United States from Manila to perform at the World's Fair. "The band has been performing for various audiences since arriving in America, and they have received great reviews for their musicianship. The conductor of the band is Walter H. Loving, a lieutenant in the American army." She pointed to a tall, handsome Negro who was positioned so that he faced the audience as he conducted. "He is a classically trained musician with a command of several instruments."

At this point a fifth guest joined our table. He introduced himself as General (retired) Allen Smythe, an American army veteran who had seen action in the Indian Wars and still exhibited a decided limp from the wound that had ended his career. He was my height, which meant that he was a few inches shorter than Holmes, but he carried a good deal of excess weight, which contributed to the pressure on his damaged leg. He leaned heavily on a cane as he greeted us with enthusiasm. He first introduced himself to the Nortons and then turned to us. "Gentlemen, it is a great pleasure to meet both of you in person. Since my retirement from the army I have served as president of the Anglo-Saxon Club in New York. Our purpose is to support, celebrate, and encourage friendship between our two great nations. I admit that I imposed on President Roosevelt to get invited to this reception so that I could meet you two gentlemen, who personify some of the most important Anglo-Saxon values — a dedication to justice and the rule of law and a reliance on reason to solve complex problems."

We were both somewhat embarrassed by Smythe's comments. But once the introductions were completed we had a pleasant evening of social interchange with the invited guests. As it turned out, Smythe was a knowledgeable opera fan who had seen several of Mrs Norton's performances. So they had much to discuss.

When the conversation came back to me Smythe asked about my military service and my experiences in India and Afghanistan. As old soldiers are wont to do, we also found time to discuss our war injuries and the battles that had resulted in these injuries — his at Wounded Knee in South Dakota and mine at the Battle of Maiwand in Afghanistan. I pointed to my shoulder and stated that it was a very reliable indicator of changes in the weather. Smythe laughed and tapped his leg with his cane. It made the sound of wood-on-wood. "I don't have any pain from the injury, but it did put an end to my career as a ballet dancer."

Smythe also attempted to bring Holmes into the conversation. After two or three unsuccessful efforts, he asked me for my opinion about Holmes' most challenging and most interesting cases. I had gotten so used to answering these types of questions that I always had five or six responses to choose from.

Holmes would later confide in me that he thought Smythe's comments about Anglo-American relations were "so much puffery" but he also admitted that he agreed with the general's basic argument. "Our two nations are in fundamental agreement about liberal values, which makes us natural allies in world affairs." I assured my friend that I completely agreed.

Our table conversation was cut off at this moment when the band began to play *El Capitan* and our attention was directed to the front portico of the White House. "Watson, I believe our host is about to make his entrance." He directed my attention to three burly and serious men who took up positions on the front steps of the mansion. Seconds later Mr Roosevelt stormed onto the White House lawn as if he were re-enacting his famous assault on San Juan Hill. He paused to enjoy the welcoming applause and then spoke: "Ladies and gentlemen, it is a great pleasure for me to welcome you all here. I am confident that you will find the occasion of your visit — the Louisiana Purchase Exposition — to be well worth the effort and inconvenience that you have had to endure in order to come to the United States. You honour us with your presence, and I look forward to getting to know each of you personally, at this evening's reception and in the days ahead." He then went straight to the first dignitary in his line of attack and without preliminaries introduced himself with an exaggerated handshake. This time the applause was much louder and more sustained.

We watched with interest as the president worked his way in our direction. Holmes said, "You will note, Watson, that the very large person who is obviously a member of Mr Roosevelt's security detail is inconspicuously informing the president of each guest's name — and perhaps other personal details — just prior to each handshake, making it appear that the president recognises the person. It is an impressive performance on both of their parts."

Approximately thirty minutes later the president finally approached our table. He was about my height, and carried more weight than he should have. He sported pince-nez glasses and a full walrus moustache. He greeted Mrs Norton first, and spent a few minutes discussing her recent performances. He demonstrated an impressive familiarity with her career and with the American opera scene in general. He then turned to her husband and congratulated him on his recent vindication in the court. General Smythe was the next to be welcomed. The president thanked him for all of his efforts on behalf of American-British cooperation.

Then Mr Roosevelt turned his attention to Holmes and me. He began to speak as he was extending his hand. "Mr Sherlock Holmes and Doctor John Watson, if I am not deceived. Even without your famous meerschaum pipe you are recognizable, Mr Holmes. Please don't stand on my behalf." He turned slightly to his left and said, "Joseph, could you get me a chair please?" With little more than a nod of his head the man signalled to an assistant, and the chair appeared. Once he was seated our host wasted no time. "Is this your first visit to Washington, gentlemen?" Without appearing to take a breath, and without waiting for a response, our host launched into an explanation of why he had requested that we be added to the list of invited dignitaries. He demonstrated a familiarity with some of my friend's more difficult cases and even made a reference to some of the cases which I had played some small part in solving. "It is clear, Doctor Watson, that you are much more than a chronicler of Mr Holmes' adventures and that he would not be here today if it were not for you." Before either Holmes or I could respond he was off again, comparing the case of Silver Blaze to an incident during one of his hunting parties in Montana. "You see, of course, that it was the absence of sound which alerted me to the danger. No bird noises, no squirrels or rabbits moving through the bush."

And all the while neither Holmes nor I had said a word. I could not help thinking that it would have been amusing to interrupt him and state, "Excuse me, Mr President, but I am the Norwegian Ambassador to the United States, and this individual is my valet." I am convinced, however, that Roosevelt would have shifted to a discussion of the singular characteristics of the Norwegian elk without missing a beat.

In time, the assault passed and the president paused in his comments. He was clearly waiting for us to say something. I assured him that we had a most enjoyable afternoon at the Smithsonian Museum. I also reported on my visit to the Gettysburg Battlefield. This last comment elicited a quick response. "Gettysburg is fascinating and historically significant, or course, but for an experienced military man such as yourself, Doctor, the Appomattox Battlefield would perhaps be of greater interest." With that, the president was off again, comparing Pickett's Charge to the Battle of Balaklava and reciting Tennyson.

The president then paused for a few moments and took a different track. "You know, gentlemen, that this house was burned to the ground by your countrymen in 1814." Holmes and I were caught off guard by this statement. It was not clear if Mr Roosevelt was expecting an apology.

But before either of us could venture a reply we were saved by Mrs Norton. "Just as you know, Mr President, that the British action was in retaliation for the burning of York, in upper Canada, by American troops in 1813."

"A valid point, Mrs Norton," laughed the president. "You have come to the aid of these gentlemen and brightened my evening as well. I did not realise that you were such a student of history, or such an Anglophile."

"Not only an Anglophile, Mr President, but a good friend of the two Englishmen with whom you are speaking."

This provided Smythe with an opening to join the conversation. "It is a comment on the wisdom of leaders on both sides of the Atlantic that, in spite of the unpleasant experiences of 1776 and 1812, they came to recognise that they shared fundamental values of democracy, free trade and religious tolerance, and that their foreign policy interests were best served by working together. Over time London and Washington have cultivated habits of cooperation that have proven indispensable to both governments."

The president nodded and said, "Indeed, General." He then returned his attention to 'the woman'. "How is it that you know these gentlemen, Mrs Norton?"

"We met in London while I was enjoying a brief respite from a demanding performance schedule. These gentlemen were kind enough to assist me with some travel arrangements." I resisted the temptation to laugh at this explanation for the circumstances surrounding our last encounter in London. We had indeed 'assisted' with her travel arrangements, in the sense that she and her husband had hastily departed from London with Holmes in hot pursuit.

I interjected, "I only regret, Mrs Norton, that you have not returned to Great Britain since that time. Is there any chance that we can lure you back for a performance at Royal Albert Hall?"

"As ever, Doctor, you are too kind. I do hope to make a European tour next year, if my husband can fit it into his schedule. In any event, I shall sing a song in your honour this evening, with our host's permission."

The president was quick to respond. "By all means, Mrs Norton, it will be the high point of our evening."

Twelve

The high point of the evening never arrived. Soon after his visit with us the president walked back to the stage which had been set up between the Constabulary Band and the White House. He positioned himself directly behind Loving, and it was apparent that he was getting ready to offer some remarks to the audience. Suddenly, two things happened in rapid succession. First, we were astonished to see Lieutenant Loving suddenly drop his baton in the middle of a waltz, lift his music stand above his head, and then fall over backwards along with the music stand. A moment later, Joseph, the president's protector, knocked Mr Roosevelt to the ground and remained on top of him.

While everyone's attention was focused on these extraordinary events, Holmes turned in the opposite direction and started to run across the lawn toward the fence on the perimeter of the White House. Although I did not understand what he was doing, I followed behind. A moment later I could see that he was pursuing a brown-skinned man wearing nothing but a loincloth and carrying a bow and quiver. The man turned back and noticed that he was being pursued, and in one fluid motion he placed an arrow in the bow and fired it at Holmes. My friend threw himself to the ground and the arrow passed over him. It landed in a sapling that was about five feet to my left. By the time that Holmes got back up the villain had abandoned his weapon and was climbing over the fence.

When we reached the fence the attacker was running to the left on Pennsylvania Avenue. "Damn, Watson, our nemesis was too fast for us. And he scaled that fence without any difficulty — not easy in the best of circumstances, but nearly impossible in bare feet." Holmes then pointed to a patch of soft ground near the fence, where an imprint of a foot was clearly visible. My friend then inspected the fence very closely and mumbled, "Just as I suspected."

Holmes and I walked back to the stage, where the president had been permitted by Joseph to stand up. About halfway back my friend stopped at a maple tree and said, "This is where the attacker hid, Watson. I assume that he was in the tree for several hours, to avoid detection by police or by the people responsible for setting up the reception." Then Holmes pointed down and I saw a deep imprint of a left and right foot. "This is where he jumped down to make his escape. We are looking for a man of considerable athletic ability and the skills of a hunter."

When we arrived back at the stage Holmes went directly to the conductor whose actions had seemed so incomprehensible. By this time Lieutenant Loving had regained his feet and was standing in front of his overturned music stand. Holmes introduced himself and offered his hand. "My compliments, sir. I suspect that your actions saved the president's life." It was at that moment that I noticed a long, thin arrow imbedded in the music stand. One member of the president's security detail bent down to inspect the arrow but Loving pushed him back. The guard's first reaction was to reach for his revolver, but Holmes intervened. "Sir, I believe that this person was acting on your behalf. Note the tar-like substance on the shaft of the arrow. If I am not mistaken, it is some form of poison, native to the Philippines."

"That is my assumption as well, Mr Holmes," Loving stated. "I suspect that it is a particularly powerful type of poison from a camandag tree, found in Southern Mindanao. The tree itself is so poisonous that simply standing under it can lead to severe illness. The slightest scratch with the milk from this tree will cause almost instantaneous death. But tell me, sir, how did you know that this poison was from the Philippines?"

"No mystery there, Lieutenant. I know from my own studies that this type of long arrow is used by the Negrito tribe in the Philippines and that they frequently coat their arrows with local poisons. It is fortunate that you were able to see the attacker from your vantage point in front of the orchestra."

Holmes then turned to the president's bodyguard and extended his hand. On closer inspection he was a mammoth of a man... fully a head taller and forty pounds heavier than Holmes. He had piercing brown eyes with a hawk-like expression of alertness. His hair was pulled back and clustered into a knot on the back of his head. "My compliments on your quick actions to protect the president, sir."

Roosevelt intervened at this point. "Joseph has been my most reliable protector for some time now, Mr Holmes. This is not the first time that he has saved my life. In fact, we first met in the Dakota Territory during the winter of '86. He found me lost and disoriented during one of the many blizzards of that year and guided me back to safety. He is the son of one of the Lakota chiefs, who gave him the name Walks Far."

During this entire introduction I noticed that Joseph's eyes focused on the hands of all of the individuals near the president. Now he looked up at Holmes and uttered his first words to my companion. "Did you see the person who attacked the president?"

"Only his back as he ran for the fence. He was wearing only a loincloth, and carrying a large bow and a quiver, both of which he threw away as he approached the fence. I recommend that you join me and Dr Watson in inspecting that area."

After he bustled the president into the White House and arranged for his protection, Joseph accompanied Holmes and me to the fence. On our way across the White House lawn Holmes pointed out the tree where the attacker was hidden, the deep footprints, and the arrow imbedded in a sapling. "Be sure to instruct your assistants to exercise great caution when they remove that arrow. I am sure that it will be coated with the same poison tar as the arrow that was meant for the president." When we reached the fence,

Holmes spoke through it to a man who was standing on Pennsylvania Avenue with a sign that read, "America out of the Philippines." The individual was startled by the size and the accusatory expression of our Indian companion, but my friend attempted to reassure him. "Sir, I wonder if you might be able to assist us. Did you happen to see a person scale this fence a few minutes ago?" After a brief pause the person responded. "I did indeed, and it was quite a thing. He was a wild native, brown skinned, nearly naked and barefoot. He landed right here in front of me, and then ran up the street." The man pointed west.

"Did you see any other persons in the area? Anyone who might have assisted this person? Did he get into a cab?"

"No, he was alone and on foot."

Holmes thanked the demonstrator for his information and requested his name and address in case there was a need for further inquiry. The sign carrier provided the information and was about to leave when Joseph stopped him. "Don't leave quite yet, sir." He then moved away from the witness and spoke quietly to Holmes. "It seems like quite a coincidence that this man has some issue with our actions in the Philippines and the attacker appears to have been a Philippine native."

"Appears is the operative word, Joseph. In fact, I am convinced that the attacker was an imposter, made up to appear to be from one of the many tribes in the Philippines." With that, Holmes took the bodyguard back to the fence and asked him to run his hand along the metal posts where the attacker had climbed. When he pulled his hand away it was coated with a brown oily substance that Holmes identified as stage makeup. "I think we can safely assume that our witness has told us what he knows, and that he is not party to a conspiracy. I think we can also conclude, however, that there is indeed a conspiracy at work here, because the perpetrator of this attack, brown skinned and bare chested, could not have gotten very far in a major American city without causing a stir. I suspect that if you extend your search for a block or so down Pennsylvania Avenue someone will report seeing a near naked man entering a waiting carriage and speeding away."

Joseph signalled for one of his subordinates and instructed him to make the recommended inquiries along Pennsylvania Avenue up to 18th Street. Holmes then asked him about the conspicuous absence of guards in front of the White House. "There is usually one policeman positioned outside the fence." Joseph pointed to a small guard post about half way along the fence. We walked to the gate next to the guard post. Joseph produced a key and we exited onto Pennsylvania Avenue. We approached the wooden guard post and stopped abruptly at the sight of a policeman crumpled on the floor. A small needle protruded from the front of the man's neck. Holmes confirmed that the man was dead and then stated, "I suspect that this dart is coated with the same poison that we found on the arrow. And the manner of his death supports my claim that more than one person was involved in this attack on the president, since the policeman was caught off guard by his attacker."

"Couldn't the person disguised as a Philippine native have killed the guard with a blow gun fired from behind that tree?" Joseph pointed to a small elm a few feet away from the guard post.

"It would have been difficult for the attacker to reach that hiding place without being noticed. And more importantly, the killer did not use a blow gun." Holmes pointed to the dart. "Note that it is slightly broken at its mid-point. This indicates that the guard was actually stabbed with the needle, which you will see is only coated with the tar-like poison on the front end. We can assume that the attacker was able to approach the guard without causing suspicion and engage him in conversation before stabbing him."

The two returned to the person with the sign and Joseph assured him that he only had one more question and then he would be able to leave. "Did you happen to see anyone over by the guard post there?" He pointed toward the wooden structure. After a brief pause, the demonstrator responded, "Well yes, I did see a well-dressed gentleman speaking with the guard. He had what looked like a map and he appeared to be asking for directions."

"Could you describe this person?"

"As I said, well dressed. I remember that he had a dark-coloured topcoat and carried a walking stick. He was heavyset, I think, and not young. He had grey hair, mutton chop whiskers, no moustache. That is all that I can say."

Holmes asked, "Did you notice if he was wearing gloves?"

"Yes, now that you mention it, I believe that he was."

Holmes turned to our companion. "An extra precaution, consistent with the proposition that the attacker stabbed your guard with the needle."

Joseph thanked the man for his assistance and asked an officer to escort him home. After he had left, Holmes spoke. "It was wise of you to ask a policeman to accompany our witness to his home. I assume that you instructed the officer to confirm that our sign carrier did indeed live at the location that he gave us."

"Quite so, Mr Holmes." Joseph then gave a series of instructions to his subordinates: To remove the policeman's body, to increase security along the fence and inside of the compound, to carefully collect the bow, quiver and arrow, and to inquire with each invited guest whether they had seen anything that might assist in the investigation. At this point the president came back out of the White House and signalled Joseph to bring us forward. Before we could speak to him, however, his protector intervened. "Mr President, you should be back inside."

"Nonsense, Joseph, I won't have my actions determined by some lunatic. I must attempt to reassure my guests." With that he charged down the steps, waving and smiling to an applauding audience. When the applause died he turned his attention to Holmes. "I am very fortunate that you were here this evening, Mr Holmes. What do you make of all this?"

"I would encourage you to take this incident very seriously, Mr President. This was not some random act by a fevered mind. This was a well-planned attack involving more than one person. The attack was also very... contrived. The perpetrators went to the trouble of acquiring an authentic Philippine weapon, and if I am not mistaken, a very rare form of Philippine poison. They did so in order to send some message regarding America's policies toward that country. I think it unlikely that we have seen the last of these individuals."

"Well then, Mr Holmes, I hope that I, and my nation, can rely upon you to assist us in eliminating this threat." Without waiting for a response, the president addressed his senior bodyguard. "Joseph, please see that Mr Holmes and Dr Watson are accorded the full support of our police and security services during their stay in our country." He then placed his hand on Holmes' shoulder and leaned forward. "I would also be very grateful for your discretion in these matters."

Joseph assured Holmes of his willingness to assist us in any way that he could, and then returned us to our table, where we were informed by Mr and Mrs Norton that the festivities had been cancelled and that all guests were being encouraged to return to their homes after speaking with a member of the president's security force. Our companions had already been interviewed by one of the bodyguards, and were preparing to leave. Mrs Norton said that Smythe had also been questioned and left. "He asked me to tell you both how much he had enjoyed meeting you." She then addressed me directly. "Dr Watson, I am sorry that I was not able to sing for you this evening, but I hope that your schedule will permit you and Sherlock to be my guests at the Metropolitan Opera during your visit." With that, the couple departed. Holmes and I soon followed them out of the reception and back to our hotel.

"An eventful evening indeed, Watson, what do you make of it all?" My friend and I had settled into the circular bar at the Willard, all brown marble and dark wood. Holmes ordered a curacao and I took the advice of our waiter to sample a cocktail called a Mint Julep (overly sweet, as it turned out).

"The attack was quite bold and unexpected. And as you mentioned to the president, Holmes, they went to a great deal of trouble to make the attacker appear to be some form of Filipino tribesman. A rifle would have been a much more effective and reliable weapon. In any event, the president is fortunate to have a very alert bodyguard and a band conductor with impressive reflexes."

"Indeed, Watson. Mr Loving demonstrated more than good reflexes. He impressed me with his knowledge of the Philippines."

Holmes paused for a moment and then continued. "And why do you suppose, Watson, that the president enjoined us not to discuss tonight's events with anyone? Keeping a lid on these developments is impossible, in light of the number of witnesses at the reception. Furthermore, the president is deluded if he thinks that he can control the press for very long. American journalists are voracious in their quest for spectacular news, and notoriously irresponsible in their willingness to divulge matters of state which the government seeks to keep secret."

"And there is a third reason why Mr Roosevelt cannot hope to keep the attack a secret. I suspect that the press will be assisted by the attackers themselves. As you yourself noted, the attackers were sending one or more messages by their attempt on Mr Roosevelt's life. Their goal was not just to kill, but to announce to the world that the killer was from the Philippines. And for his part, I can only assume that the president's sensitivity on this issue indicates that he is embroiled in some ongoing foreign policy matters that he wishes to keep confidential. Tomorrow we will need to educate ourselves about American relations with the Philippines."

With that, Holmes finished his cocktail and I left my half-finished Mint Julep, and we both retired to our suites.

After all of the evening's excitement it was several hours before I was able to sleep. When we met to go down for breakfast the next morning Holmes said nothing but I knew that he too was awake late into the night, since I could hear him quietly playing his violin. At one point I thought that I picked up bits of Mendelssohn's violin concerto in E minor.

After we were seated in the hotel's restaurant Holmes handed me a copy of the New York Times, with the headline: "Filipino Terrorist Attempts Assassination." "As I expected, Watson, news of last night's attack could not be suppressed."

The article that followed stated that the editorial office of the newspaper had received an unsigned letter claiming credit for the attack and stating that more such actions would be forthcoming if the United States did not abandon its efforts to occupy and control the Philippines.

Thirteen

Hastings arrived promptly at two p.m. to escort us to the train station. After the porter guided us to our overnight cabins and deposited our luggage, we met in the bar. Holmes decided to use this occasion to ask our host about America's relations with the Philippines. Hastings paused for a few moments to collect his thoughts, and then provided us with what sounded like the official Department of State pabulum. "America is engaged in a great experiment in the Philippines, Mr Holmes, bringing democracy to a population that has only known tribalism and the repressive rule of Papist Spain. After we ejected the Spaniards from Manila our government began an ambitious campaign of benevolent reforms to put the Filipino's on the path toward self-government. But some Filipinos who had a stake in preserving their dominant positions in that country whipped up public resistance, which required us to pursue a campaign of self-defence and containment. By the time that President Roosevelt replaced President McKinley most of the military resistance had ceased, but America still faced strong opposition. Only now the opposition was here at home, where misguided individuals have unfairly compared our efforts in the Philippines to the forms of immoral imperialism exercised by many European governments. These people forget that we acquired the Philippines by treaty and by payment. What the president's critics seek is not an end to American expansion. It is contraction, and the betrayal of the tradition of Manifest Destiny that has guided our nation for over a century."

Holmes could not resist putting Hastings on his back foot. "I assume you count Britain among those immoral imperialist nations?"

"I have the utmost respect for your great nation, Mr Holmes. Your countrymen are our natural allies in the advancement of civilization. Indeed, there is no better argument for America's mission in the Philippines than your Mr Kipling's poem about the 'white man's burden'. I admit, however, that I was shocked by some of the tactics that your armed forces employed during the recent campaign against the Boers."

The American press had been very critical of the British management of the Second Boer War. But our government had invited some of this criticism, first by its overestimation of the ease with which British forces would be able to suppress the opposition from a group of Afrikaner farmers and then by the policies subsequently employed by our troops. In the end, we had to rely upon scorched earth strategies and the use of concentration camps to contain, and ultimately conquer, the Boers. The war contributed to a dispirited public mood in Britain, that was compounded by the passing of our great Queen Victoria at the height of the conflict in Southern Africa.[2]

I intervened at this point to steer our conversation in another direction. "Holmes, I believe that you and I should repair to the dining car. I am sure that Mr Hastings has some important foreign policy business to attend to."

"Indeed, Watson, we would be well advised to enjoy an early dinner and then an early retreat to our sleeping compartments. Tomorrow promises to be a busy day."

The dining car was elegant, with mahogany tables and window frames, green velvet seats and sparkling place settings on lace table cloths. Once we had ordered I stated that I hoped I did not offend our young friend by not inviting him to join us. "I wanted to solicit your opinions about our host, Mr Roosevelt, and I thought that this would place Hastings in a difficult position."

"I agree, Watson. But let me begin by asking you for your first impressions of the American president."

"Well, as you know, I read many of his speeches and writings in preparation for this trip. They reflect a preoccupation with Spartan themes and values... honour, courage, the will to conquest. He is a hunter of some skill,

---

[2] As I read my comments on the Boer War I am reminded that not everyone shared the view that Britain had acted inappropriately in its campaign to control the Afrikaners. I encourage the reader to refer to an important pamphlet by Dr Arthur Conan Doyle: *The War in South Africa: It's Cause and Conduct*, which paints a very different picture. I was recently informed that this publication was the main reason why Dr Doyle was awarded a knighthood by His Royal Highness.

apparently, and he makes much of the myth of the American cowboy. Our brief meeting with him at the White House did nothing to undermine these impressions. I might add that his personality seems ideally suited for a still-young nation that is seeking to establish itself as an economic, political and military colossus."

"I agree with your general assessment of the man, Watson, although I suspect that I am less confident than you are about the beneficent role that Mr Roosevelt will play in the world. History provides us with numerous examples of the darker side of such highly ambitious leaders. Today in Japan the themes which you associate with Mr Roosevelt have been adapted to the cult of the Bushido, which has fuelled aggression against many of Tokyo's neighbours, including Russia, China and Korea, and could spread beyond the Pacific."

"You must admit, Holmes, that you are making a very great leap — I would say, a quite unjustified leap — from the idealism of President Roosevelt to the barbarism of the Japanese."

"Perhaps you are correct, Watson, and I do our host a disservice. But I also direct you to the president's own words. While I was in New York I purchased a copy of one his books, titled *The Winning of the West*. Some passages were startling for their aggressive tone. He asserts, for example, that 'the most ultimately righteous of all wars is a war with savages, though it is apt to be also the most terrible and inhuman.' He lists the American wars against Indians as an example of this type of necessary conflict. I wonder how he can reconcile this type of rhetoric with his expressions of admiration for the red man in general and for his Indian companion Joseph in particular." Holmes paused for a sip of his claret and then concluded, "I will withhold judgment until I have acquired more information."

I was about to comment on what I had learned at the Carlisle Indian School when my friend said, "Allow me to shift our conversation to the Louisiana Purchase Exposition. By now you must be Britain's expert on the subject."

I welcomed the opportunity to offer some comments on the World's Fair. I had been following press reports of the festivities in Saint Louis. I had also purchased a small tour book which included information on the major exhibits at the fair, along with maps of the fairgrounds. "As you know, it is a celebration of the centenary of the so-called Louisiana Purchase, Thomas Jefferson's acquisition of a vast tract of land west of the Mississippi River. Napoleon had acquired the territory from Spain in 1800 as a significant expansion of the French empire. By 1803, however, he was coping with a slave revolt in Saint Domingue and preparing for another round of war with England. Jefferson moved quickly to take advantage of these circumstances to strike a deal with the French Government. With this one action the president more than doubled the size of the United States at a very modest cost of fifteen million dollars. The Louisiana Purchase Exposition is envisioned as a celebration of this important stage in America's westward expansion. But it is also designed to put other nations on notice that the United States has achieved the status of a world power and that its ambitions and its influence would henceforth extend across both the Atlantic and the Pacific oceans. And as I have stated, Mr Roosevelt seems ideally suited to lead this nation toward empire — if he can be kept alive."

On that sombre note we completed our meal and retreated to our sleeping compartments.

Fourteen

We arrived in the Saint Louis Union Station in late afternoon. Hastings informed us that it was the world's largest and busiest train station. He arranged for our luggage to be forwarded to our hotel, curiously named the Inside Inn. Hastings explained that the name referred to the fact that the hotel was actually located within the grounds of the World's Fair. He then escorted us to a busy restaurant within the station, where we had a serviceable, and long overdue, lunch. Our host explained that the timing of the late afternoon lunch was fortuitous, since we would be arriving at the Fair at sunset.

While we ate, Hastings gave us some information on Saint Louis. "It was founded by fur traders on the western banks of the Mississippi river in the late 1700s, and it became part of the United States in 1803 as a result of the Louisiana Purchase. It was the starting point for Lewis and Clark's expedition to chart the territories acquired by the purchase. For the next several decades Saint Louis served as the 'gateway to the West', as well as an important trading and industrial centre. Immigrants flooded in, first from Germany and Ireland and then later from places like

Italy and Greece. By 1890 it was America's fourth largest city."

When we had finished lunch Hastings flagged a four-wheeler and instructed our driver to take us to the main entrance to the fairgrounds. When we reached our destination we exited the carriage to take in the view.

Hastings had done his research. "The first thing that catches your attention, gentlemen, is the Louisiana Purchase Monument, topped by a statue of Liberty Astride the Globe. The body of water behind the statue is the Grand Basin, which leads to the Cascades and to Festival Hall, the location for most of the large musical events at the fair. It is equipped with the largest pipe organ in the world."

As he was speaking the entire complex was beginning to be electrically illuminated, which gave everything a three-dimensional effect. A building on the right side of the Grand Basin was especially bright — like one enormous electric bulb. Hasting's explained that the building was, appropriately, the Palace of Electricity.

Both Holmes and I would have been content to admire the spectacular scene in silence, but of course our guide could not be restrained. "The fairgrounds cover an area of approximately one thousand two hundred acres, with a midway — called the Pike — which is nearly a mile long. There are approximately one thousand five hundred buildings to hold all of the exhibits."

When neither Holmes nor I made a comment Hastings said, "What do you think? I hope that you agree that there has never been anything like it. It makes both the Paris Universal Exposition of 1889 and the Chicago Columbian Exposition of 1893 seem like county fairs." When he again received no response he invited us to return to the carriage and directed our driver to take us to the Inside Inn which, Hastings informed us, "Was the largest hotel in the world, with over two thousand two hundred rooms, a staff of more than two thousand, and the largest kitchen in the world." He continued his monologue as we travelled along the periphery of the fairgrounds to our hotel.

The lobby of the Inside Inn was both enormous and chaotic, and not at all welcoming. Hastings confirmed our reservations and then bid us farewell, with a promise to meet us the next morning for a tour of the World's Fair. We were greeted enthusiastically by the night manager, who assured us that we had been given two of the finest suites in the establishment. Getting to those rooms proved to be a daunting task, however. We followed the bellman for fully fifteen minutes, up flights of stairs and along corridors before arriving at our rooms. We then met in my suite to discuss next steps.

As he lit his pipe, Holmes observed that "young Hasting's fascination with the size of things, whether it is train stations, hotels or world fairs, confirms one of the familiar clichés about Americans. But this establishment is a reminder that great size does not insure quality. I would propose that we go downstairs for a light supper and a cocktail, but I fear that we might never find our way back to these rooms."

We agreed to order sandwiches and American beer from room service and then settle in for a quiet evening. We rang for a bellman and asked for a menu. "If it's sandwiches that you want, you might try hot dogs. They are all the rage at the fair." He explained that they were made of ground beef and pork, rolled together and placed in a bun. "When a fellow named Feuchtwanger first sold them it was just the sausage. He would loan people gloves to keep their hands clean as they ate. But some people did not return the gloves. When he complained about this to his wife, she recommended that they place the sausage in an open bun. Most folks eat them with yellow mustard and sauerkraut." In spite of the name we were intrigued, and ordered one each with our beer. When they arrived, along with a small container of mustard and a bowl of sauerkraut, we both took a cautious bite, starting at one end of the bun and then making our way to the other. As we became more confident we experimented with the mustard and sauerkraut.

"I must say, Watson, I enjoy the flavour of this hot dog, and I also like the convenient design of the round 'dog' and the surrounding bun." We were less impressed with the beer, which was called Falstaff and made by the local Lemp Brewery. It was too thin and too cold for our British palates.

After our brief meal we retired to our rooms to read some of the brochures and maps that the concierge had provided, to prepare us for our visit to the World's Fair. These materials served as an excellent complement to the information that I had already acquired. The packet included a special edition of the local newspaper, the *Saint Louis Post-Dispatch*, which celebrated the opening day of the fair: 'Attendance, estimated 200,000; Previous Record, Philadelphia, 186,672' (once again, size above all things). The centrefold of the newspaper provided a detailed map of the fairgrounds, which would prove to be indispensable over the next few days.

Fifteen

I awoke very early the next day, still adjusting to the disruptions of travel. I was tempted to remain in bed, but chose instead to use this opportunity to reconnoitre. After completing my ablutions I grabbed my small guide book and left the inn. It was nearly two hours before the fair opened, and most of the people whom I saw were workers who were preparing the exhibits. I started walking east, past a cluster of buildings each of which celebrated one of the American states. I entered the beautifully maintained Sunken Garden and then followed the path that took me behind Festival Hall, the white marble centrepiece of the fair. I spent some time admiring this building, which, I read, had a dome that was larger than Saint Peter's Basilica.

My next stop was the Great Wheel, one of the most popular entertainments at the fair. I was fortunate that a worker was testing it out when I approached. He explained, "It was built by George Ferris for the Columbian Exposition in Chicago and then shipped here for our Fair. It is two hundred and fifty feet tall and takes a full fifteen minutes to complete one rotation of the thirty-six cars." For a small compensation he allowed me to ride in one of the cars. I had an initial feeling of nervous discomfort as the wheel began to lift me above the fairgrounds. But my qualms disappeared as the fair opened below me. I looked down on the fountains which were distributed around the Grand Basin, the electric trolley cars which were beginning to transport early morning visitors around the periphery of the fair, the artificial lake that hosted naval battles twice each day, and the great Floral Clock. When my car reached the apogee of the Great Wheel I could see the full sweep of the fairgrounds. I was awestruck, and I promised myself that I would share this experience with my friend before we left Saint Louis.

By the time that I got back to the Inside Inn my legs ached. I met Holmes for breakfast and then rested in my room until we joined Hastings at noon. I chose not to inform him of my early morning outing, since I did not want to disrupt the plans that he had made.

Our afternoon began with a meeting with David Francis, the president of the board that oversaw the fair. After introductions, Hastings departed, citing, "State Department business." After a few cursory comments about the popularity of the fair, Francis stated, "But I realise that you are not here as tourists. We have been contacted by a member of President Roosevelt's security staff, who has informed us that you are here to assist us in insuring the president's safety during his upcoming visit to the fair. We are happy to provide whatever help you require." He then introduced us to Edgar Rhymes, head of security for the fair. Francis bid us "a productive afternoon" and then departed. Rhymes explained his plans for the next two days. "Gentlemen, as you know, we have very little time before Mr Roosevelt's arrival, so we will only be able to skim the surface of the fair. Today I would recommend that we begin with a general orientation tour of the fairgrounds. This will take the entire afternoon. Then after an early dinner I would propose that we spend some time in the Philippine Reservation, since I have been advised by the president's Indian bodyguard that this exhibit is of particular interest to you."

We were encouraged by Rhymes' straightforward manner and immediately agreed with his recommendations.

The next few hours were exhausting. The fair was enormous and we were constantly being jostled by a relentless tide of humanity. The crowd was particularly boisterous along the Pike, with young people running from one entertainment to the next and people attempting to eat and drink while they were on the move. At one point I came close to colliding with a young man who was eating something that Rhymes described as an "ice cream cone." Rhymes explained, "It was invented here at the fair, when an ice cream vender ran out of cups. His friend who was a baker gave him a piece of pastry and showed him how to wrap it so that it could carry a scoop of ice cream in one hand. They are even more popular than hot dogs."

As we made our way along the Pike, Rhymes pointed out some of the entertainments, including Under and Over the Sea, where guests are given the illusion of traveling to Paris in a submarine and then returning to the United

States by airship. The Temple of Mirth subjected visitors to one hundred and fifty distorted mirrors and a three-story slide called the Helter Skelter. Christian guests can choose between The Hereafter, where they can travel through Dante's Inferno before exiting in Paradise, and Creation, where they can experience the first six days of the Book of Genesis. "If guests don't mind getting soaked, they can Shute the Chutes — a ride in a small open boat down a two hundred and fifty-foot-long ramp into a pool of water. Guests can also watch a trained elephant slide down the ramp into the pool."

While Rhymes continued his commentary we were constantly pushed back and forth by the visitors to the Pike. The only time that the crowd stopped moving was when everyone's attention was drawn to an airship which drifted lazily over our heads. Mr Rhymes informed us that it was a popular attraction at the fair. "It competed in the aerial concourse which took place about a month ago. Four types of aerial transportation attempted to manoeuvre around a number of balloons. Unfortunately, none of the competitors were capable of accomplishing this feat in the required minimum speed of fifteen miles per hour, so no one won the grand prize of one hundred thousand dollars. It was nonetheless quite a spectacle for guests who were fortunate enough to be at the fair at that time."

Rhymes pointed upward. "This particular airship was entered into the contest by a German inventor, Count von Zeppelin. After the concourse ended he decided to keep it here for the remainder of the fair. I have had the distinct pleasure of riding in it... an exhilarating experience. It provides the best view of the entire fairgrounds — except, perhaps for that." He pointed to the slowly turning Great Wheel that dominated everything else in its surroundings.

Sixteen

As we made our way across the fairgrounds we came upon a small group of tourists surrounding what could only be described as a monstrosity — a machine that was fully ten meters tall and appeared like nothing so much as a giant metal insect. As we approached, Rhymes pointed. "It is called a Pyreliophorus... also known as a sun machine. It is really quite something. It is a solar furnace, comprised of over six thousand mirrors that can concentrate the sun's rays and generate a focused beam of seven thousand degrees Fahrenheit. It was awarded the grand prize among all of the inventions at the fair. Allow me to introduce you gentlemen to the inventor." Rhymes led us to a young man in a priest's garb and collar who shook our hands. "My name is Father Manuel Gomes, but most people call me Padre Himalaya. Thank you for your interest in my Pyreliophorus. I was just getting it prepared for a demonstration, but I will be happy to answer any questions that you might have before we get started."

Holmes was clearly intrigued by the device, and immediately began to pepper the priest with detailed questions. "Is it necessary to adjust the mirrors before every demonstration? What is the range of the beam? I assume that the heat dissipates very quickly as the target moves away from the furnace? How is it that a Roman Catholic priest is engaged in this research? Do you see any practical applications for such a device?"

Gomes was pleased by Holmes' questions. "Yes, the mirrors demand frequent and careful adjustment. And you have put your finger on one of my biggest challenges — finding a way to concentrate the beam at a distance of more than twenty meters. As to your question about my dual identity as a priest and a scientist — I have always believed that we do God's work when we seek to expand human knowledge. I am fortunate that my archbishop in Lisbon shares my belief that religion and science are two paths that lead to the same destination. He has seen fit to release me from my priestly duties so that I can continue with my research. And in answer to your last question, I cannot claim that my invention has, or will have, any practical applications, unless it proves useful in large scale destruction projects such as the removal of a steel bridge. And now, if you will excuse me, my audience is anxious for a demonstration."

Gomes walked to the back of the machine and tinkered with some controls. The huge device began to turn slowly on a circular base and then to tilt so that the narrow end of the device was aimed at a small target — a block of iron ore which had been placed on a flat stone at a distance of about ten meters. When it stopped the priest pulled another lever, which removed a cover from the top of the machine, opening it to the sun's rays. The audience waited in silence for a couple of minutes and was then rewarded with a truly remarkable demonstration, as the iron block began to glow red, and then orange, and then began to melt, leaving nothing in its place except for a molten puddle. We joined the guests in loud applause, and then congratulated the scientist-priest and took our leave.

Rhymes led us to a restaurant on the eastern side of the fairgrounds, where we enjoyed a much-needed rest during dinner. Our meal was not memorable, but we greatly enjoyed the entertainment that was provided to the diners. A person named Will Rogers, who was advertised as 'the lariat and chatter man' sat on a stool in the middle of the room, dressed in full cowboy regalia. He spoke casually while absent-mindedly twirling his rope. At one point, he expanded the lariat in size and completely encircled a table with two guests. Rogers entertained his audience with humorous comments about American politics. "I am not a member of any organised political party. I am a democrat. It's a good thing we don't get all the government we pay for." When he finished his performance he came directly to our table. "It is good to see you again, Mr Rhymes." Our host introduced us and I was quick to compliment him on his performance. Rogers responded with what was clearly a practiced comment, "There's no trick to being a humourist when you have the whole government working for you."

Rogers pulled a chair to our table, sat down and asked about our opinions of the fair and Saint Louis. After a few minutes of casual conversation he was joined by an individual who patted him on the back and said, "Good show tonight, Will. You have to teach me how to do that trick with the lariat."

"Gentlemen, this is my friend Samuel Clemens, better known as Mark Twain." With his distinctive bushy hair and eyebrows, drooping moustache and white linen suit, our new guest needed no introduction. Handshakes around. Twain expressed great admiration for my friend's career and for my ability to bring Mr Holmes' adventures to life. I reciprocated by stating that his publications have provided me with many hours of enjoyment, but I admitted that I had felt a great deal of sympathy for the European tour guides that he tormented in *The Innocents Abroad*. "I remember that at one point you admitted that you took this action 'merely for the pleasure of being cruel'."

"Quite so, Doctor. And I do not regret my actions. These charlatans paraded us through every gift shop in their country, and I am sure that they invented most of the historical details that they burdened us with. They are fortunate that I limited myself to verbal attacks…"

Then I made the mistake of mentioning that we were planning to visit the Philippine Compound that evening. Twain bristled at this comment and then said, "I refuse to visit what can only be described as a human zoo. I have criticised my government's assassination of the liberties of these innocent people. Washington just wants to be like the aristocratic countries of Europe, with their possessions in foreign waters. I know that I am in the minority with these opinions, and that I am up against the pulpit, the press and the public. But so be it."

His passionate comments elicited an uncomfortable silence, which was fortunately broken by our waiter presenting the bill. We excused ourselves and extended our best wishes to both Clemens and Rogers.

We left the restaurant just as the lights began to come on across the World's Fair. From there, it was a short walk to the Philippine Compound. Rhymes explained that it was one of the most ambitious, and one of the most popular, exhibits at the fair, and that its creation had been a high priority for the Roosevelt administration. "The idea came from Secretary Taft, when he was governor-general of the Philippines. He made a strong case that an exhibit which introduced fairgoers to aspects of Philippine society would be a powerful repost to the naysayers like Mr Twain who are opposed to America's civilizing mission in the Pacific. The exhibit is designed to encourage optimism and excitement about the economic, political, and military benefits of Philippine-American cooperation."

As we approached the Philippine Compound we were attracted to some lively martial music. We followed the sound across a long foot bridge over a lake that separated the compound from the rest of the fairgrounds and entered an open area that Rhymes explained was a replica of the Plaza Santo Tomas in Manila. In the centre of the complex chairs were distributed around a stage, which was illuminated by dozens of electric lights. I was pleased to discover that it was a performance by the Philippine

Constabulary Band that had entertained us at the White House. We immediately recognised Lieutenant Loving, the tall, handsome American Negro officer who may have saved the president's life by his quick actions. Loving was in full command of his orchestra, waving his baton and signalling various musicians with a nod of his head. We found three chairs and settled in to hear the performance, which was a tribute to the American composer and conductor John Philip Sousa.

Only a few minutes had passed when all of the lights in the plaza went dark. The audience gasped and the orchestra was temporarily silenced. But within seconds Loving had reached into his jacket and removed a white handkerchief. He tied it to the end of his baton, said a few words to the musicians, and resumed the performance at precisely the point at which it had been interrupted. At the end of the song the band was rewarded with thunderous applause. Loving continued to conduct in the dark for a few more songs, the handkerchief seeming to float of its own accord in front of the orchestra. He closed the program with a rousing performance of Sousa's "The Invincible Eagle".

After Loving accepted congratulations from members of the audience he joined us at a small table in the plaza. Fortunately, it was lit by a small candle. The lieutenant greeted us enthusiastically and it was clear that he and Rhymes needed no introductions. All three of us congratulated him on his handling of the disruption.

Holmes asked, "What did you say to your musicians when the lights went out?"

"I reminded them that this is what we practice for, and informed them that we would take it from measure thirteen and complete the program as scheduled."

"Most impressive, Lieutenant. This is the second time that you have demonstrated an ability to respond quickly and effectively to a crisis. You have also demonstrated very impressive conducting skills. Can I inquire about your musical training?"

"I studied the cornet and conducting at the New England Conservatory in Boston and then continued my musical studies in Vienna, before joining the army."

"And you have risen to a position of great responsibility as head of the Philippine Constabulary Band. I would imagine that your experiences in the Philippines have given you a unique perspective on American relations with that nation. Might I ask for your views on this relationship?"

"I can speak as a musician and as an American citizen." Loving paused for a moment and then said, "I should state that my comments are my own, and do not reflect the opinions of the United States Army.

"As a musician, I consider myself to be extremely fortunate to be able to work with such innately talented performers. With the support of Governor-General Taft I was able to recruit the very best musicians in the archipelago. The governor-general was also instrumental in getting us invited to the fair and to a number of locations outside of Saint Louis including, as you know, the White House. My job here requires me to perform both an entertainment function and a policing function. With the help of my band members I am expected to keep the Philippine natives in line and in their compound. It is an interesting assignment, which would be much more difficult if it were not for Mr Rhymes and his staff.

"Speaking as an American, I am very supportive of our efforts to establish a permanent presence in the Philippines. With seven thousand islands stretching from north to south in the Western Pacific, the Philippines are the key to our long term 'Open Door' strategy. Have you gentlemen read the works of Admiral Mahan?"

All three of us said no.

"He makes a powerful argument for America's future as a Pacific actor. He supports the Open Door in the form that the term is usually employed — as an economic argument in favour of American competition with European and Asian nations to insure that we have a fair share of the trade and investment opportunities in the Pacific. But Mahan goes further, asserting that America must be prepared to exercise its military muscle in Asia in order to insure that the Open Door remains open. The Philippines certainly provides us with economic opportunities, but the islands are even more important as an unsinkable base for our army and navy. From that platform we will be able to influence, and intimidate both the rising Asian actors like Japan and the ambitious

European powers like Russia, Germany, and if I may say so, your great nation."

At this point Rhymes congratulated Loving once again for the concert and asked him if he would be available to accompany us the next day on our tour of the Philippine Compound. Loving agreed to meet us at the entrance to the compound at ten a.m. Rhymes then stated that Holmes and I should probably return to our hotel. We agreed with this proposal, since both Twain and Loving had given us a great deal to think about.

When we were settled in the hotel bar I pressed Holmes for his opinions on the fair.

"An exercise in national chest thumping, Watson. But I have to admit that it is very impressive."

"I agree, and I am intrigued by the way that the American government has taken advantage of the fair to generate support for its policies in Asia."

Holmes nodded. "I will reserve judgment on that issue until after we have visited the Philippine Compound tomorrow."

Seventeen

Our cab delivered us to the main entrance of the fairgrounds at nine the next morning, where we met Rhymes. He had advised us that we would need a full hour to get to the Philippine Reservation on foot, since the fairgrounds were so large, and we would need to allow for the crowds that would impede our progress. Our path took us past massive buildings that celebrated America's accomplishments in such fields as transportation, machinery and agriculture, then past the great Observation Wheel and the Floral Clock and finally to the footbridge that we had crossed the night before. Rhymes pointed out a building on the edge of the lake. "That is the Indian School, which our organisers chose to place opposite the Philippine Compound to contrast the sad state of a dying Indian civilization here in America with the great future that awaits the people of the Philippines with American guidance and support."

I informed him that I had visited the Carlisle Indian School recently, and that I had been very impressed. I also made a note to ask Joseph for his views on Rhymes' reference to a 'dying civilization.'

The compound was on the northern edge of the fairgrounds. We met Loving at the entrance to the foot bridge and our group made its way across the lake. Rhymes began his tour, noting, "The plaza is surrounded by four villages, which house nearly one thousand two hundred natives. Some of our nation's most prestigious scientists helped to design the compound, as a living tableau. While emphasizing the potential of the more advanced tribes, the organisers did not shy away from exhibiting some of the most backward peoples as well."

"The anthropologists who designed this complex chose four tribes to illustrate the great diversity of the Philippines. The Negritos are the most savage — small in stature and low in intellect. According to Mr Darwin's theories they are on a path to extinction. The Igorots are also quite primitive, but there is still hope that they will be able to take advantage of American tutelage. The Moros are the next level up on the social hierarchy, but they practice the Mussulman religion and are not always welcoming to our fairgoers. In fact, we have had to post signs warning guests not to attempt to take photos of these people and to engage them at their own risk. The fourth village is the home to the Visayans, the most civilised of the Philippine natives. You will see that they wear clothing that would be acceptable in an American town. They are also on the path to becoming the wealthiest people in the Philippines, since they have already become proficient at silk weaving."

I asked if the Visayan village was the most popular exhibit in the Philippine Reservation.

"Unfortunately, no. By far the most popular exhibit in the compound is the Igorot village. Most of the people who visit it are there in the hope of witnessing the Igorot's habit of feasting on dogs. The preparation and consumption of the dogs by the Igorots has become one of the most popular diversions at the fair. For many guests, this exhibition fuels negative impressions of the Philippines as a country of savages, but hopefully this is offset by the other exhibits in the compound, which encourage optimism about the future of Philippine society."

By this time, we had in fact reached the first of the villages, where a Negrito native was demonstrating his proficiency with a bow and arrow. I recognised the bow as identical to the one used during the reception at the White House. As we watched, a fairgoer positioned himself about twenty paces from the archer and held out a nickel between his thumb and forefinger. I noticed that he closed his eyes as the Negrito archer launched his arrow and knocked the nickel from his hand. The audience applauded as the native collected and pocketed the coin.

The demonstration reminded us that we were not here as tourists. Holmes asked Loving if he or any of his Constabulary members had heard anything about the incident at the White House since their return to Saint Louis. "The local papers have made a great deal of noise about a Filipino being responsible for the attack. But neither I nor my troops have encouraged the press in this regard."

"Have there been any other noteworthy developments among the Filipinos recently?"

"Some fights among natives, and some unpleasant interactions between Filipinos and fairgoers, but nothing very serious and nothing unexpected."

After a pause, Loving continued. "The only thing that might be worth mentioning is the disappearance of six natives since our arrival in Saint Louis. When we made our initial plans for the trip to the United States we allowed for the chance that a handful of natives would be tempted to scale the walls of the compound. But where would they go, with no money, no English, and almost no clothing? We concluded that any brave soul that attempted such an escape would be back in his village by the next morning. So the extended absence of these natives is a bit of a mystery."

These comments seemed to pique my friend's interest. He turned to Rhymes and asked if he had heard of any other missing persons among the thousands of employees and exhibitors at the Fair.

"Now that you mention it, there have been some unexplained absences from both the Japanese and the Chinese pavilions. But these individuals are attending the Fair as representatives of their governments, and unlike the Filipino natives, most of them are culturally, linguistically and financially at ease in our nation, we simply assumed that they had chosen to leave the Fair for a variety of mundane reasons. We have not considered the possibility that these cases were related to the Philippine disappearances."

Holmes said, "Indeed, and it strikes me as more than coincidental that all of the people who have gone missing are Asians. Mr Rhymes, would you be so kind as to inquire with representatives of the Japanese and Chinese exhibits about the details of these disappearances? Who are these individuals? When, precisely, did they disappear? What type of work did they do at the fair? Where are they from in Japan or China?" He then turned to Loving. "Lieutenant, would you make similar inquiries among your Filipino contacts?"

Holmes then caught us all by surprise by stating, "Watson we must now leave these gentlemen and pursue another line of inquiry." With that, we said goodbye to our guides and Holmes proposed that we meet the next day for lunch at the Restaurant Pavilion in the centre of the fair.

Eighteen

Holmes led me at a fast pace across the fair. At a certain point I caught up with him and said, "I say, Holmes, why are you in such a rush?"

"I don't want to be late for our appointment, Watson. Here, this should explain it all."

Holmes handed me an envelope with a note inside that was entirely numbers:

13 1597
28657 3 6765 4181 121393
21 233 46368 196418 2
21 6765 55 28657 28657

"I assume this is some kind of numerical code, Holmes. Are you able to decipher it?"

"Elementary, Watson. I recognised immediately that these numbers are all part of the Fibonacci sequence, named after an Italian mathematician from the thirteenth century. Each number in the sequence is the product of the two preceding numbers. So: 1, 1,2,3,5,8,13 and so forth. This simple code uses Fibonacci numbers to correspond with letters in the alphabet. But to make it a bit more interesting the author has reversed the alphabet, so that the last letter, the Z, corresponds to the first number of the

Fibonacci sequence, the one. It took me only a few minutes with pencil and paper to break this particular code. It reads:

UK

Exhib

Today

Three."

I suddenly realised that we had arrived at the entrance to the Great Britain Pavilion. Holmes bounded up the steps and I followed. There was a modest crowd inside, looking at various examples of British innovation and enticements to British tourism. Holmes walked across the great hall to a security guard posted in front of a door.

My friend said, "I believe we have an appointment." And without uttering a word the guard opened the door and ushered us inside. By this time I had figured out who we would be meeting, but I was still astonished to see Holmes' brother seated in a chair in the centre of the room. Always corpulent, he seemed to have grown larger since our last meeting, but he still had the same expression of intense, concentrated intelligence.

I spoke first. "Greetings, Mycroft, I never thought that I would see you outside of your Diogenes Club."

With great difficulty, Holmes' brother lifted himself out of his chair in order to shake my hand. "It is not my club, Dr Watson, in the sense that I do not own it. I am, of course, a founding member." Mycroft then turned his attention to Sherlock. "Thank you for coming. I am glad that you were able to decipher my message."

"Childs play, Mycroft. The only part that gave me a moment's pause was the reversal of the sequence so that the first became last and the last became first, as the evangelist Matthew would say."

"Not my best effort, but I was in a bit of a rush, and had no reason to believe that the note would be scrutinised by anyone but you. Now, to business." Mycroft indicated two chairs that had been placed in front of him by an assistant.

"I assume that you are here to provide us with more information on the threat to President Roosevelt."

"Yes."

"And how long have you been in the United States?"

"I arrived a week before the presidential election. My purpose was to oversee precautions designed to protect Mr Roosevelt and to gather intelligence. Most of my time since my arrival has been spent in the British Embassy in Washington, in discussions between our security staff and their counterparts in the American Secret Service."

Holmes asked if the American contingent included Joseph Walks Far. "He has led the United States delegation." I took note of the fact that Joseph had made no mention of his meetings with my friend's brother. I was reminded once again of the tangled web which was Mycroft's world.

"Our government must have had a very strong indication that the president's life was at risk to justify asking you to make this arduous journey."

"Indeed." Mycroft removed an envelope from the inside pocket of his suit jacket and handed it to Holmes. The document was obviously very brief, because it only took Holmes a few moments to read it.

"I assume that this memorandum comes from reliable sources within our intelligence services." Mycroft confirmed this with a brief nod. "And I assume that this is a very important new development from the point of view of Number 10?" Again, the nod.

At this point, without further comment, Holmes handed me the missive, dated November 20, 1904. It stated:

President Roosevelt has begun secret discussions with representatives of the Government of Japan regarding the preconditions for a mutual defence pact. The president appears to be prepared to formally recognise Japanese sovereignty over Korea in exchange for Japanese acceptance of American occupation of the Philippines. The president is also pressing both Tokyo and Moscow to accept his mediation of the ongoing Russo-Japanese War. To date, the Czar has rejected this offer, both because he is still optimistic that Russia can win the war in the Pacific and because he suspects (probably correctly) that if Roosevelt is permitted to host the peace talks he will favour Tokyo. But the momentum in the war has clearly shifted in Japan's favour, and Moscow may soon be confronted with a choice between an unfavourable peace treaty concocted by Washington or a humiliating defeat.

For this reason we believe that the threat to the president has greatly increased. If Mr Roosevelt can be eliminated it will bolster the influence of the anti-imperialists in Washington and make it more difficult for America to pursue an ambitious foreign policy in the Pacific.

When I was finished reading the document I said, "This is interesting, but why did you feel it was necessary for you to deliver it in person?"

Mycroft reached into his jacket pocket once more, and extracted another piece of paper. "Because of this. We have one advantage over the Russians. They do not know that we have a photo of the likely attacker." He handed the picture to Holmes. "We believe that this is the man who disguised himself as a Filipino native and attempted to kill the president at the White House. We assume that he will be one of the people who will make the attempt on the president's life here in Saint Louis."

"How did you come by this picture?"

"We have been monitoring the activities of a member of the Russian Embassy staff whom we believe to be the person directly responsible for organizing the attack on Mr Roosevelt in Washington. We believe that he is the person who killed the policeman at the guard post. We assume that this person also provided the carriage which the attacker used in his escape. For the last couple of days we have followed this individual when he has been outside of the embassy, and on two occasions he has met with this person." Mycroft pointed to the photo.

"This should help us to prepare for the attack… assuming that we are correct about when and where it will take place."

Mycroft nodded. "Mr Roosevelt has arranged for the head of his security detail to meet with you tomorrow to discuss special arrangements for the president's safety during his visit to the fair in two days." With that, Mycroft rose — with some effort — to leave. "If you have any additional questions, I can be reached through Lionel, who will be here at the British Pavilion." He gestured to his assistant and then moved slowly and with visible discomfort to a rear door. Holmes and I turned in the opposite direction and exited.

Nineteen

Joseph Walks Far met us for breakfast the next morning at our hotel. By this time we had acquired enough familiarity with the hotel so that we could manoeuvre between the bars, restaurants and our rooms.

"I am pleased to see both of you gentlemen again, but I admit that I am uncomfortable serving as part of the president's advance detail rather than traveling with him."

Holmes responded that while we could sympathise with his desire to be with Mr Roosevelt, we were very reassured by his presence. My friend then presented Joseph with the photo of the suspected assassin.

"I will see to it that all of my agents are provided with a copy of this picture. Should we also distribute a version of this picture which presents the assailant disguised as a Filipino native?

"I don't think that will be necessary," Holmes replied, "since the crowds at the World's Fair are so large. The attacker would draw too much attention to himself in a loin cloth and darkened skin."

Joseph nodded. "But tell me, how did you acquire this drawing?"

I was not surprised when Holmes demurred. "I hope that you will accept our assurance that this is an accurate rendering of the individual who attacked the president at the White House. We are not at liberty to go further in explaining how we came by this picture. Nor can we be certain that this person will make another attempt on the president's life while Mr Roosevelt is at the fair."

"Very well, Mr Holmes. I will not press you at this time. In any event, I am fairly certain that I know the identity of the individual who provided you with this picture. He is a person of great... gravitas." Both Holmes and I suppressed our smiles.

"I will be busy today organizing the security detail and tracing the path that Mr Roosevelt will take tomorrow. For your information, he will be arriving at about noon and will begin his visit with a luncheon with members of the Louisiana Purchase Exposition Company. He will then proceed to the Louisiana Purchase Monument, where he will make some brief remarks before joining you two gentlemen and other invited guests on the reviewing stand in front of Festival Hall, where there will be a parade in his honour, followed by his formal speech. His duties will end with a visit to the Philippine Compound to attend a concert by the Constabulary Band."

Joseph then addressed the issue of security. "I will have men deployed at each of these locations, including one man placed in a gondola at the highest point on the Great Observation Wheel. He will be equipped with a telescope and a red flag. If he spots the assassin he will signal with the flag to assist us in locating this individual. I have also instructed the other members of my team to carry red handkerchiefs. If one of my men spots the assassin in the crowd he will raise the handkerchief above his head and we will converge on that point. Now gentlemen, I must excuse myself. I will be meeting with Mr Rhymes to make final plans for the president's security. Let me propose that we meet here for dinner this evening, so that we can discuss last minute details."

Holmes rose to bid our colleague goodbye. "Your plans make good sense, Joseph. We have a meeting this morning with Lieutenant Loving, to discuss the president's visit to the Philippine Compound. I am anxious to acquire some additional information on this exhibition, since the person who attacked the president in Washington went to the trouble of disguising himself as a Filipino native."

After completing our breakfast we hired one of the many automobiles provided by the Saint Louis Car Company. We were both impressed by the comfort and the quiet of the machine, which deposited us at the Bridge of Spain that connected the Philippine Compound to the rest of the fair. Lieutenant Loving was waiting for us, along with a strikingly handsome young woman, with dark brown eyes and an athletic figure. "Gentlemen, let me introduce you to Miss Maria del Pilar Zamora, who is in charge of the Model School in the compound. She can provide you with many insights about the purpose and functioning of the Philippine Compound." We introduced ourselves and thanked her for taking the time to meet with us. I then asked her to tell us a bit about her duties at the fair.

"I came to the United States from Manila, as one of two teachers of the Filipinos at the fair. I never met the second teacher, who died of pneumonia when he arrived in Saint Louis. I am kept very busy, teaching the children traditional topics — Geography, Arithmetic, English — in the morning and then helping adult tribe members with their English in the afternoon."

Miss Zamora's reference to pneumonia was of interest to me. "Have there been many deaths due to illness among the various tribes?"

Miss Zamora spoke as we crossed the bridge and entered the large open area that we had visited earlier. "I know of several cases, and I have been informed that before the Filipinos arrived in America, plans were already in place for a significant number of deaths due to differences of climate and susceptibility to local diseases. I was also told that arrangements had already been made for the bodies of these Filipinos to be sent to major museums and universities in the United States, for research purposes. This has made people very upset, since our traditions of burial are sacred to us."

There was no mistaking the criticism in Miss Zamora's comments, but her passion made her appear even more attractive to me.

When we reached the centre of the Plaza Santo Tomas, Loving pointed out where the band would be performing the next day, and where the president would be positioned in the square.

Holmes asked if there had been any notable incidents in the compound.

Miss Zamora spoke first. "You may have heard that about a month after the Filipinos arrived in Saint Louis it was discovered that some of the Igorots were climbing over the walls at night and hunting for dogs." The young teacher did not attempt to disguise her disgust as she spoke.

"Yes, we were informed about this. We were also advised by the lieutenant that six Filipino natives have escaped from the compound. Have there been any further developments in this regard?"

Loving confirmed that the number had now grown to eight, and that a few people were still missing from the Japanese and Chinese exhibits. "To date none of these individuals have returned and none have been found outside of the fair."

"Very curious," said Holmes, "and disturbing. Nothing is more troubling than a seemingly important anomaly for which there is no apparent explanation." My friend then settled onto a bench beneath a large dogwood and began to fill his black clay pipe.

I recognised this behaviour and invited Loving and Miss Zamora to join me for lunch. "Mr Holmes will not be fruitful company for the next couple of hours." Indeed, I had known my friend to consume a full ounce of his harsh shag tobacco while working his way through a particularly complicated mystery.

Loving informed us that he had another appointment and we said our goodbyes. I admit that I was not disappointed that I would have Miss Zamora's exclusive company for lunch. She led me to a small café within the Philippine Compound. As we were being seated, I made the mistake of attempting to inject some humour. "Will the menu include any canine dishes?"

Miss Zamora's expression made it clear that I had overstepped. "No, Doctor, and I can assure you that only a very small portion of Filipinos engage in this behaviour."

My attempt to impress this attractive woman had backfired. I apologised for offending her, and then tried to salvage the conversation by asking her for her views on America's purpose in bringing nearly one thousand two hundred Filipinos to the fair. I stated that Mr Rhymes had informed us that Washington was interested in developing an exhibit that would celebrate the potential for American-Philippine cooperation and convince people that Washington should retain control of the archipelago. "Is that the paramount rationale for the compound?"

"That is one of the goals, but there is another... entertainment. The organisers of the fair felt that by exhibiting Filipinos in what they believed to be their 'natural habitat' they would draw crowds and generate profits. They created a Department of Exploitation to make decisions about the clothing the Filipinos would wear, the weapons that they would carry, and the ceremonies in which they would participate. The most outrageous example of this cultural interference was the decision by the organisers to actively encourage the Igorots' preference for dog meat. Once it was discovered that the natives were hunting for dogs at night a deal was struck. If the Igorots would stay in their compound, the city of Saint Louis would provide them with dogs from the local pound." She looked to me for a reaction.

"I see the problem," I said. "The president and his advisers imagined that by introducing fairgoers to these exotic peoples, and reassuring them about the potential for at least some of the tribes to evolve into productive members of society, they could tip the scales of public opinion in favour of a long-term American occupation of the archipelago. But once they were ensconced here in the compound some of the tribes began to engage in activities that fairgoers viewed as either repulsive or salaciously intriguing. In either case, the result has not conformed to the White House's expectations."

"Quite so, Doctor. I will be glad when this experiment is ended, and I and my compatriots can return to our homes."

We completed our lunch and then returned to the square where Holmes was still furiously smoking his pipe. "I confess that I am still confounded by the disappearance of so many individuals, and all of them Asians. If they were all taken against their will, then to what purpose, and why were so many needed? With your permission, Watson,

I will remain here and continue to reflect on this conundrum. I will see you back at our hotel this evening."

I was about to bid farewell to Miss Zamora when it struck me that I might not see this beautiful young woman again, and I did not want our only interaction to end on a negative note. "Miss Zamora, would you be willing to join me for tea?" I was a bit surprised when she agreed. We walked back across the bridge and found an attractive restaurant which faced the Floral Clock.

We were looking for a convenient table when we were intercepted by a waiter. "I am very sorry, but all of our tables are reserved."

I did not understand, and I began to point to various empty tables. "Surely all of these spaces cannot be reserved…"

I was about to ask to see the manager when Miss Zamora placed her hand on my arm and said, "Please, Doctor, I cannot afford to be involved in an incident." As she led me out of the restaurant I noticed that she was attempting, without success, to hold back a tear. "I am sorry, Doctor, I should have realised the risk of going out of the compound. Lieutenant Loving and I have discussed this issue, and we agree that we must avoid these types of confrontations for the sake of the Filipinos who depend on us. We have already had one cautionary incident — some members of the Constabulary Band made the mistake of leaving the compound to enjoy some of the entertainments along the Pike. They narrowly escaped lynching."

As she spoke, Miss Zamora led us back across the footbridge and into the compound. We ended up at the same café where we had lunch. After we were seated I said, "I am so sorry for placing you in that situation. I should have throttled that waiter."

"He was just acting on behalf of the management, and I would suspect, the majority of the fairgoers." Then she laughed. "I am a fairly light skinned person, but I am frequently reminded since I arrived in this country that I am not light skinned enough…"

I felt the need to apologise for my entire race. Instead, I spontaneously reached across our table and placed my hand on top of hers. I noticed that she looked around to be sure that my action had not set off an alarm, and then she rewarded me with a radiant smile.

"Please call me John."

"Very well, John, and you may call me Maria."

It was at this moment that our waiter arrived. After we ordered we continued our conversation. Maria spoke about her experiences growing up in Manila, her decision to pursue a career in teaching, and her impressions of Philippine politics and society. I told her about my experiences as a military doctor and the circumstances that led me to pursue my very strange career as a chronicler of my friend's adventures. I also told her about my two marriages. The time passed very quickly, and when it was necessary for me to leave I told Maria how much I had enjoyed our time together and expressed the hope that we could see each other again.

"It was indeed a pleasure to get to know you, John. If circumstances permit, I would welcome the opportunity to see you again, although the incident at the restaurant this afternoon is a reminder of the limits that society has placed upon our friendship."

With that last cautionary comment, Maria once again placed her hand on my arm and said goodbye.

Twenty

I met Joseph Walks Far for dinner that evening as planned. Holmes had decided to stay behind to learn a bit more about the Filipino tribesmen and the Philippine Compound. I was happy for the opportunity to hear Joseph's account of his experiences at the Carlisle Indian Industrial School. I told him that I greatly enjoyed my visit to the Indian School. "I was impressed by their efforts to provide educational opportunities to so many of your brethren." It was clear from Joseph's reaction that I had struck a nerve. When he finally spoke, he chose his words carefully.

"As you know, it was due to Mr Roosevelt that I was sent to Carlisle. He viewed his invitation to attend the Indian School as a reward for my help when he was lost in the snow. I brought him to my tribe, where he stayed until the storm passed and it was safe for him to return to his hunting camp. While he was with us, he became a close friend of my father and a year later he sent a message, inviting him to send me to the Indian Industrial School. I did not want to go, but my father ordered me. He said, 'These people are like a great wave that is pushing us farther and farther away from the land of our ancestors.

The wave cannot be resisted. But you, and others like you, can join the white man's world and help our people to survive.' He had heard stories about what happened to Lakota people at the Indian School — that we would be forced to wear white man's clothing, speak the white man's language, and even cut our hair. He instructed my mother to cut my hair before I left for the school, to save me from the shame of having it done by a white man. Both my mother and I cried while she did as he instructed.

"The first year was the hardest. As you may know, the slogan of the school is: 'Kill the Indian and save the man.' There were many times when I felt like I was being killed, slowly. I hated the clothing that we were compelled to wear — the starched collars, and worst of all, the red flannel undergarments. I wanted to return to my people, but my father would not permit it.

"Life at the Indian School became easier after I learned English and joined sport teams. I particularly liked football. We played against schools like Harvard and Yale. Most of our opponents were bigger than us, but we were tough, and we developed some tricks. When I knocked someone down I always offered a hand to help them back up. They usually refused, but I like to think that, in later years when these people thought about Indians, they would remember both being put on the ground by one and being offered a hand back up."

I then asked Joseph about his relationship with the president.

"He has been like a second father — supportive and encouraging. From time to time he asks for my opinion about an issue or policy that affects the tribes. His decision to make me the head of his security force was unpopular with some members of the government and with members of the Secret Service. But he seems not to have given this decision a second thought."

I asked Joseph about the president's views on Indians.

"Mr Roosevelt is proud of the westward march of America, but he also knows that this expansion has been at the expense of the tribes. He is like a Lakota in his concern for the earth... he loves to be out among the plants and animals, and away from cities. Last year I went with him and a man named John Muir to visit the great sequoia trees and the Yosemite area. We camped for three nights. At one point we had to make our way through four feet of snow. The president compared the giant trees to the columns supporting Europe's great cathedrals. He said that the natural beauty of the area was more wonderful than those man-made buildings. He has talked with me about his plans to make more national parks like Yellowstone, and I have helped him to find good locations for these parks."

"So you have gone very far in accomplishing the task that your father set for you."

"I hope that I have made some small impact, but I cannot predict how the next president, or his successors, will deal with issues that affect Indians. When Mr Roosevelt leaves the White House I plan to return to my people and to use the things that I have learned in Washington to help them. I will marry a Lakota woman and live according to the old ways, while using my knowledge of American law and politics to defend our interests. I do worry, however, that by the time I am ready to return to my tribe I will no longer remember how to be a Lakota. I already find myself searching for words in my own language."

I was tempted to offer some reassurance, but I realised that it would sound insincere, or even patronizing. So I kept my silence. We both focused our attention on dessert — ice cream, of course — and then went our separate ways. We agreed to convene at the train station the next morning, to meet the president and his entourage.

Twenty-One

The president's special sleeping car arrived on time and was welcomed by an enthusiastic crowd. The Constabulary Band played "Hail to the Chief", preceded by the traditional ruffles and flourishes. As soon as the song ended the president appeared at the rear of the train, waving his hat and smiling broadly. I was reminded of the comment by his daughter Alice that the president 'wanted to be the bride in every wedding and the corpse in every funeral.' After making a few general remarks Mr Roosevelt signalled to me, Holmes and Joseph to join him in the train. Joseph wasted no time once we were inside. "Mr President, we have increased the size of your security detail for this visit, since you will be very exposed at certain times." He handed the president a piece of paper. "Here is your itinerary. I would ask you to resist the temptation to diverge from this plan."

The president nodded, but it was not clear if this was a sign of agreement or simply a way of cutting short this line of discussion. "But tell me, gentlemen, how is the fair?"

Our delegation exited the train and boarded a line of automobiles, similar to the one that we had used the previous day. We moved slowly across the fairgrounds so that the president had an opportunity to waive to the crowds. We arrived at the U.S. Government building, where the president was ushered into his lunch with the local dignitaries. This first stage in the festivities went off without complications. Our parade of automobiles then transported us a short distance to the Louisiana Purchase Monument. The president took his place under the shadow of the statue of Liberty Astride the Globe and prepared to make his remarks. Those of us who were responsible for his security were now on very high alert, and referring to our copies of the photo of the suspected assassin. At that moment we saw the agent that Joseph had placed at the top of the Great Wheel. He had picked up a red flag and was waiving it furiously. Then he pointed the flag downward and in the general direction of the president. Almost immediately, a hand waving a red handkerchief went up in the crowd very near to where Holmes and I were standing. We started to move in that direction, when we heard a shot and the handkerchief disappeared. Hysteria ensued, and the president was unceremoniously hustled back into his car and driven away.

Holmes and I ran forward and found one of Joseph's agents lying on the ground bleeding from a chest wound. He had a pistol in his right hand, which Holmes removed. We paused for a few moments to get our bearings in the hysterical crowd, and then a second shot was fired and we began to run toward the sound. The attacker had fired into the air to clear a path for himself. We passed a number of people who were screaming and running in fear.

The criminal was much younger than us, and we could never have caught him on foot. Fortunately, one of the automobiles that was designated for the president's visit was still nearby. Holmes commandeered this vehicle and directed the driver to follow the individual who had fired the shots. He was still visible, running in the direction of the Pike. We followed until our prey looked back and saw that we were still in pursuit, at which point he ran into the nearest exhibit, The Hereafter. We exited the automobile and followed our prey inside. We were temporarily disoriented by hundreds of mirrors that surrounded us. Holmes pushed forward to the person who was dispensing tickets. He informed us that a man waving a gun had run past and taken the slide to Hades — he pointed into the dark and we went forward. At the top of the slide another attendant confirmed that the man with the pistol had used this mode of escape. When Holmes said that we needed to pursue this person we were each given a small straw mat and instructed to sit with our arms wrapped around our knees. We were pushed down the ramp by the attendant. I admit that this was quite frightening, particularly since I had no idea if I would meet a bullet when I arrived at the end of my trip.

When Holmes and I reached the bottom of the slide we were greeted by darkness and loud wailing coming from all directions. One light played on a sign above my head: 'Abandon all Hope ye who enter here.' With our guns drawn we took a few cautious steps forward and came to a body of water with a man in biblical garb standing knee deep. Holmes said, "If I remember my Dante, this would be the Acheron, the body of water that separates earth from Hell, and you, sir, would be Charon, the person who conducts doomed souls to the underworld."

"You are right, mister, but right now I am just a man who had his boat stolen by some bastard with a gun."

"We are in pursuit of this individual. Is there another boat that we can use?"

"The man pointed behind him at a vehicle that was similar to ones that I had seen on railroad tracks. "You face each other and pump the cross bar up and down. The boat that that bastard stole has only a small electric motor. If you work at it you two can catch him with this."

We climbed onto the vehicle and began pumping up and down. Getting started was difficult, but with some effort we began to make progress.

The designers of this 'inferno' did not attempt to reproduce all nine levels of Dante's hell. But they did select some of the more famous. We first passed through the second circle — lust — where I saw Francesca of Rimini and her lover Paolo locked in a tormented embrace, flying over my head. They were pursued by her husband Giovanni who was screaming and waving his sword at the lovers.

We next entered the sixth circle, where those who were guilty of wrath were condemned to furious battle with each other, for all eternity. I tried to block out the screams and the moaning, and not be distracted by the tumult around me. This became easier to do after we spotted our quarry up ahead.

A few minutes later we entered the eighth circle, where simoniacs are punished for selling ecclesiastical favours. Their punishment was to be placed upside down in holes, with their bare feet exposed to constant fire. Although the moans of these sufferers were not nearly as loud as the cries of the wrathful, they were actually more disturbing. When we were about halfway through the eighth circle a mannequin of a skeleton wearing a priest's garments leapt out at us, screaming. I was fortunate to be holding the crossbar, which saved me from falling into the water.

Seeing that we were closing the gap, the assassin turned back and fired his pistol in our general direction. But with all the chaos and darkness around us I had no reason to be concerned. At this point he decided to abandon his boat and wade through the shallow water. We stopped our vessel and pursued him. When we reached dry land we began to chase our prey through the forest of naked legs, kicking and twisting in agony. The sole of each bare foot was topped by artificial flames. Holmes and I ran as fast as we could while avoiding the flailing legs. I was not entirely successful, and suffered a painful kick to my right hip. I was able to continue my pursuit but Holmes was several strides ahead of me. We could see the assassin making his way through the kicking legs to a small door in the back. We chased him through the door and down a flight of steps which led us to the ninth circle of Hell, where we were confronted by the three headed ruler of the Underworld, who roared at us and spit fire from his mouths. I could actually feel the heat, but Holmes and I continued to keep our focus on our quarry. He looked around and then ran to another small door that was behind the fire-breathing Devil. As he ran through the door he turned and fired his pistol again, but once again his aim was completely off.

The door on the ninth level opened to the outside, and at first the sunlight was blinding. When we regained our sight I realised that we were still on the Pike. I saw our quarry turn to the right and enter an exhibit identified as Hagenbeck's Zoo. Once again, he fired his gun in the air to clear a path. We followed him through a gate that opened onto a large area full of exotic animals. I took note of llamas, alpacas, kangaroos, and even a panda bear. They scattered as the assassin ran past them to another small gate. He was through it quickly and running down a steep hill by the time that we got to the gate. I saw him run into another body of water which reached up to his waist and then I saw him look up and to his left. At that same moment I heard hundreds of voices screaming in unison and then I realised why. Our prey had run into the Shute the Chutes at precisely the moment when the trained elephant was making his daily slide into the manmade lake.

It was over in a matter of seconds. The animal appeared to be as frightened as our quarry, and after they collided the elephant raised his trunk and bellowed, and then ran across the lake to two handlers who were able to subdue it.

When Rhymes arrived he argued that we should downplay the incident to the extent possible. "We cannot completely disavow the attack, but we can assert that it was an attempted armed robbery that ended with the death of the perpetrator."

The next morning's papers did not question this version of events, but one journalist tested the limits of decorum by printing a one-word headline: "Pachidermination!"

That night at the hotel bar it required two brandies to relax. Before we went to our suites Holmes said, "When you describe today's events in your account of this case, Watson, I hope that you will resist the temptation to emphasise the more grotesque details of our 'chase through Hell.'"

Twenty-Two

In spite of the libations I was still agitated when I said good night to Holmes. I tossed in my bed much of the night and was not fully rested when I met him for breakfast the next morning. I did not inquire about his night, since I knew that after the many adventures of the day he would not, could not, sleep at all. I have always marvelled at my friend's ability to remain awake and alert for long periods while working on a particularly challenging case.

"Watson, you will not be surprised to hear that Mycroft has requested that we meet him this morning. We know that the person who attempted to kill the president did not act alone, and we also know that he was an agent of, or at least in the employ of, the Russian Government. I assume that my brother wishes to discuss next steps."

We met Mycroft in the same room in the Great Britain Exhibit. "Congratulations to both of you gentlemen. I have been informed by Mr Rhymes of your exploits yesterday. He mentioned that the attacker had been armed with a Nagant M1895, a standard issue revolver for the Russian imperial army and police forces. This is not surprising, but it is also not implicative. Fortunately, we already know the identity of his superior in the Russian Embassy, and we do not require definitive proof in order to take action. I will be leaving for Washington on the three o'clock train today, and I would be grateful if you gentlemen would accompany me."

After a quick lunch we checked out of our suites. We met Mycroft and his body guard at the Saint Louis train station, but once we were on board we did not see Holmes' brother again during the trip. Holmes and I met for an early dinner and then retired to our sleeping compartments. We arrived in the nation's capital at midday and took a carriage to the Willard Hotel. Once again we took advantage of the hotel's proximity to the Smithsonian complex to make a return visit to this impressive network of museums and art galleries.

We met Mycroft for dinner at the Willard that evening. He informed us that his agents had identified the man who had attempted to kill the president as an American career criminal named James Powell. They were also able to provide information on his superior. "Grey hair, mutton chop, middle aged, his name is Vladimir Penkov. He serves as head of security at the Russian Embassy. This afternoon I sent him a message, asking him to meet me in Lafayette Square Park in front of the statue of Andrew Jackson this evening at ten. I added an enticement — that I needed to discuss an article that is about to be published in the Washington Post. I would be grateful if you would join me for this meeting, Sherlock, and you as well, Dr Watson." He then informed Holmes of the role that he wished him to play. He also asked if my friend still had the pistol he had taken from the Secret Service agent who had been killed in Saint Louis. Holmes confirmed that he still had the weapon and that he would bring it to the meeting that evening. I advised Mycroft that I would also bring my Webley.

Penkov was punctual, a sign that he took seriously Mycroft's reference to a newspaper article. After introductions the Russian asked, "How can I be of service, gentlemen?" He then turned to my friend. "And to what do I owe the honour of a meeting with the famous Sherlock Holmes?"

Mycroft responded, "I asked my brother to join me today so that he could provide you with the details of Mr Powell's death."

Penkov began to speak but was cut off by Sherlock. "Please don't waste our time with claims of ignorance. I was witness to Powell's last words. He expressed a sense of shame for having attempted to kill a fellow American and he specifically mentioned you as the person who had paid him to take this action." Penkov paused for a moment and then said, "I have been a diplomat long enough to recognize a pack of lies when I hear them, Mr Holmes. I think this conversation is at an end."

At this point, Mycroft took over. "I regret that you have taken this position, Mr Penkov, but I cannot say that I am surprised. I also realise that you have diplomatic status and therefore cannot be prosecuted in this country. That is why I brought this along."

Mycroft reached into the outer breast pocket of his coat and removed a bright blue pocket handkerchief. He looked around to confirm that we were still by ourselves in the park and then he removed a small, pearl-handled Remington two-shot pistol from his right coat pocket. In one smooth motion he covered the gun with his handkerchief, placed it under Penkov's chin, and fired. The Russian collapsed at our feet.

All three of us looked around again to be sure that there were no witnesses. Then Holmes said, "I was wondering about that bit of silk in your pocket. I have never known you to opt for such an affectation."

"I brought it along to muffle the sound of the gun and to wipe my finger-marks off if I was forced to take action." He looked down at the corpse and then said, "Our Mr Penkov appears to have been an unfortunate example of a man who was driven to suicide by the demands of his profession."

I noticed that neither of the Holmes brothers seemed in the least bit upset by the man's death.

By this time we were beginning to attract some attention. A couple who appeared to be out for a late-night stroll came toward us. I took the initiative to state that I was a physician and began to fumble with the corpse. I positioned myself in such a way that the couple could not see the wound under the man's chin. After a few minutes I pronounced him dead. "He appears to have suffered a massive heart attack." Holmes then informed the couple that the police had been summoned. That was enough for the onlookers, who continued on their walk.

I was more concerned when a policeman approached. I realised that there was no use in claiming that Penkov had died from a heart attack, so I was silent. The officer knelt next to the corpse, looked up at Mycroft and said, "Greetings from Mr Walks Far. I see that this gentleman has had a terrible accident. I will take charge of this situation." As he was speaking I noticed that a police wagon had pulled up nearby, and another officer was walking toward us.

We took our lead from Mycroft, who said nothing. He wiped the gun with his silk handkerchief and handed it to the kneeling officer, who placed it in the right hand of the dead Russian. Then Mycroft placed the handkerchief back in his pocket and departed. We followed him out of the park and returned to our hotel.

Twenty-Three

On our way back to the hotel Holmes informed me that he had agreed to meet Mycroft for lunch the next day at the restaurant in the Ebbitt House Hotel so that his brother could inform us of his meeting that morning with the Russian ambassador. I was pleased to have the opportunity to eat at this establishment, which had a reputation for the best Blue Point oysters in Washington.

The restaurant was impressive, with seating for over two hundred guests, crystal chandeliers, rich linens and fine china. Although more than half the tables were occupied I was immediately struck by the silence. No loud laughter here and no raised voices. This was a place for doing deals that could not be overheard. With its high-backed chairs, it brought to mind the atmosphere of the Diogenes Club.

Mycroft was actually smiling as he approached our table — something that I found more than a little disconcerting. He ordered a bottle of champagne to accompany the molluscs and then began his account of his meeting with the Russian ambassador, Leonid Ivanov.

"The meeting was a lovely piece of theatre, with two actors reciting lines that they both knew to be nonsense. I began by assuring Ivanov that I was there as an old friend, to help him with a difficult situation. I told him that I did not for a minute think that he had any knowledge of or involvement in the two attacks on the American President. I assumed that he was conducting his own investigation into this matter, and I had asked for this meeting so that I could assist him in this regard. I extracted a folded piece of paper from my jacket pocket and handed it to him. I informed him that although I could not explain how I came by it, the document was incontestable.

"It took Ivanov only a minute to scan the note, which I had helped Joseph Walks Far to construct. It was a brief message from the Secret Service agent to Vladimir Penkov, in which Walks Far confirmed that a second payment of one thousand dollars had been deposited in his bank account, as payment for his assistance in the prevention of two attacks on Mr Roosevelt.

"I informed Ivanov that I would not have provided him with this memo if Penkov was still alive and acting as an American asset. But since I had heard that Penkov had committed suicide I saw no reason why I could not help the ambassador with his inquiries. Then I sank the hook, by pointing out to Ivanov that the memo was undated and that he could use it in any way that he saw fit, as long as he did not identify me as the source. It took him a moment to understand why I had pointed out that the memo was not dated. Then I noticed a slight smile on the ambassador's face, and I knew that he realised that the absence of a date allowed him to claim that he had received this information while Penkov was still alive. This meant that he could also claim either indirect or direct responsibility for Penkov's execution. I guessed that he would assert that he had personally fired the shot. This would help Ivanov to silence his enemies in Moscow who would be looking for a way to blame him for this double fiasco. It might even enhance his reputation as a 'take charge' individual.

"I know the ambassador well enough to predict that he will not risk any further attempts on the president's life now that he is directly in the spotlight. I would have preferred to see him punished for his complicity in the two attacks on Mr Roosevelt, but sometimes we have to settle for half of a loaf, and in this case the priority is an outcome that is likely to keep the president safe."

Mycroft paused to consume another oyster and then concluded, "It is also nice to know that the ambassador understands that he owes me a very large debt, which I can collect at any time in the future."

"So," Holmes stated, "both you and the ambassador knew that the attacks on the American president could not have occurred without his direct involvement. But you are applying Sun Tzu's dictum to keep your friends close and your enemies closer."

Mycroft nodded and then took a last sip of his champagne. As he rose to leave us he said, "I am pleased that, with the completion of this task, I can now return to England. I assume that you gentlemen will also be returning to London now that your duties are completed here in America?"

My friend replied, "We intend to spend a few more days in New York before our departure. Watson and I are looking forward to attending the concert by our friend Mrs Norton at the Metropolitan Opera House."

At this point I shook Mycroft's hand and wished him safe travels. "When we are back in London perhaps we can find an occasion to meet — to share another bottle of champagne…"

Holmes' brother simply responded, "Indeed," but without any apparent interest.

Then Mycroft surprised me by leaning close to Holmes and taking his hand. He whispered in Sherlock's ear and I noticed that my friend stiffened and stepped back. Mycroft left without another word.

"What was that about, Holmes?"

My friend replied, "After all these years, my brother still does not know me. He felt compelled to warn me that Irene Adler was now beyond my reach as Mrs Norton."

Holmes simply shook his head as we exited the restaurant.

We returned to the Willard and were surprised when the receptionist presented Holmes with a telegram. My friend scanned it and then gave it to me. It merely said: *Two more Filipinos missing from compound.* It was signed by Loving. "Watson, I am afraid that we will have to endure another overnight train trip to Saint Louis. Our duties at the fair do not seem to be finished."

Holmes sent a message to Walks Far, informing him that we had been called back to Saint Louis and would not be available to assist in protecting the president until further notice. We then contacted Hastings to inform him of our change of plans. Ever the reliable factotum, he offered to make the necessary reservations on the night train for Saint Louis which was scheduled to leave in two hours. He apologised for not being able to join us, citing "important State Department duties." I was tempted to ask him if his duties included lessons in ordering pasta and wine in Italy, but I restrained myself.

We rushed to collect our luggage, check out of the hotel, and hail a hansom. We arrived at the Baltimore and Potomac station in time to settle into our sleeping compartments.

Twenty-Four

Hastings had telegraphed ahead, and Loving was waiting for us at the Station. "Gentlemen, thank you so much for making this strenuous train trip yet again. I hope that I have not wasted your time by drawing you back to Saint Louis."

Holmes assured the conductor that he had used good judgment. "The fact that there have been so many disappearances, that they have all been Asians, and that to date none of these individuals have been found is ample reason for further investigation."

"I am glad that you feel this way," Loving responded, "and I may have a lead for us." He flagged down a brougham and climbed onto the seat with the driver. Holmes and I sat inside, with blankets on our laps. The carriage took us back to the Inside Inn. Loving instructed the driver to wait for us. He guided us through the ever-present chaos in the lobby to the reception desk, where he waited for us to check in and leave our luggage with the bellman. Loving then led us back to the waiting carriage and instructed the driver to take us to the Philippine Compound on the north side of the Fair. When we arrived at the footbridge Loving guided us to the Model School within the Philippine Compound, where Miss Zamora was waiting for us. I made no attempt to disguise my pleasure at seeing her once again. When I shook her right hand she placed her left on my arm and rewarded me with a smile.

Then she spoke to Holmes and me. "Welcome back, gentlemen. Lieutenant Loving has informed me of your concern for the missing Filipino tribesmen. I share this concern, of course. As you know, very few of the Filipino natives know more than a few words of English, and virtually all of these individuals are intimidated by the world outside of the compound. This is why I share the lieutenant's opinion that these natives did not leave the Fair voluntarily. But how and why were they kidnapped?"

"I may have a partial answer to this question," Loving said. "Three days ago I was speaking with a Bontoc Igorot named Olo. He was very excited. He had met with a man from the outside who was known as 'dog man' because he is the person who has been authorised by the Department of Exploitation to provide the Igorots with dogs. On a weekly basis he delivers about ten dogs to the Igorots. He comes at night, in order to avoid public scrutiny or interference and he is admitted to the compound by the Philippine Scouts who are on duty. Over the last few months he has acquired an elementary command of the tribal language of the Igorots. On this occasion he informed Olo that he had come into possession of an extra twenty dogs, and that he would be willing to give them to the Igorots for their ceremonies and public events for one dollar per dog. As you have heard, the cooking and eating of dogs is one of the most popular exhibitions at the fair, and the primary source of income for these natives. So they stood to make a great profit from the additional animals. The dog man informed Olo that, because the animals had been stolen from Saint Louis citizens, the transaction would have to take place at night, and in secret. He also told Olo that he would need to recruit another Igorot to assist him in transporting the dogs to the kennel, located in the Igorot village. He assured Olo that the guards at the entrance to the compound had been paid to look the other way during the operation. This was all supposed to take place two nights ago, and I have confirmed that Olo and one other member of the Igorot tribe by the name of Antonio have been missing from the compound for the last two days."

Loving informed us that he was acquainted with this dog man. "He is employed as a dog catcher by the city of Saint Louis. Because the city fathers are somewhat embarrassed by their arrangement with the Igorots this individual is encouraged to carry out his duties in secret. So he is in an ideal situation to engage in illegal activities."

The lieutenant then put forth a plan. "Later today I will meet with the commanding officer of the Philippine Scouts, Major William Johnson. I will inform him of what we know about the missing Filipino natives and request that he arrest and keep incommunicado the two Scouts who were on guard duty two nights ago, so that they cannot warn the dog man that he has been discovered. Then later this afternoon we will position ourselves outside of the city pound, along with two of my most trusted members of the Constabulary Band. We will follow the dog man when he leaves work. Our next actions will be determined by where the dog man goes. Hopefully he will lead us to the location where Olo and Antonio are being held captive."

Holmes and I agreed with the plan, although my military experience had taught me to always be sceptical. There was every chance that we would not find the dog man at the pound, or we would find him leaving work but he would not lead us to the two Igorots. Or perhaps we would follow the dog man to the place where Olo and Antonio were imprisoned, but we would find ourselves out manned and out gunned. This last thought made me reach into my great coat pocket to touch the handle of my revolver. As if he was reading my thoughts, Holmes reached into his pocket and extracted the pistol that had belonged to the Secret Service agent who was killed at the fair. He confirmed that there were four shots in the revolver and returned it to his coat pocket.

Loving left us at this point, stating that he would meet us later that afternoon. We returned to the Inside Inn and had our luggage brought up to our rooms. I allowed myself a too-brief rest until Loving knocked on my door. He was accompanied by two sergeants whom he introduced as Alejandro Reyes and Cesar Cruz. I was reassured that they were both NCOs, since it meant that they probably had some experience with combat. I noticed that they were both armed with Krag-Jorgensen rifles which had served American troops very well during the recent war with

Spain. I remembered that this weapon had two significant advantages. It carried a five shot magazine and it was smokeless, so that an infantryman did not give away his position when the weapon was fired. I also noted that Loving was armed with a Colt 1889 model double action revolver, which the lieutenant reminded me was the same weapon that Mr Roosevelt had carried when he led his Rough Riders up San Juan Hill. "What is more important, Doctor, is that it is a reliable hand gun with a very powerful punch."

Holmes was ready when we knocked on his door, and our group started out for the dog pound in a barouche that was driven by Sergeant Cruz. We arrived before five and settled into a hilly area that gave us both camouflage and a good line of site on the pound. We did not have to wait long. The dog man, whom we had been informed by Loving was named Amos Rivers, left the pound on foot shortly after five. We left our carriage and followed him at a distance on foot. He followed a path for about a mile through a relatively isolated area, arriving at a dilapidated building which had once been some type of warehouse. Rivers entered by a side door. We approached carefully and positioned ourselves at a window. In spite of the grime we were able to see Rivers inside. He went directly to a small office at the front of the building. He was gone for a couple of minutes and then exited the office dressed in a white gown with a hood, a mask, gloves and eye covers. He walked to the back of the poorly lit warehouse and disappeared.

As soon as we stepped inside the building my olfactory nerve was violently assaulted. I had not experienced such smells since my service in the overcrowded field hospital in Afghanistan. I pointed to the small office that the dog man had just vacated, and led by our two sergeants with their rifles at the ready, we went inside. The stink was not so overpowering here, thanks to two open windows.

I was pleased to see several sets of protective gear stacked on a table in the corner of the office. I also saw hypodermics and vials containing some form of clear liquid in a small glass cabinet. I whispered to my colleagues that we should don the protective costumes, as the dog man had done. We proceeded to assist each other in dressing. I also noticed that there was a jar of menthol on the table. I dipped my finger into the ointment and rubbed it between my upper lip and my nose, to mask the oppressive stench. All of my companions did likewise.

When we were prepared our sergeants led us out of the office and toward the rear of the warehouse. As we approached we could hear moaning and coughing, which should have prepared us for the sight that confronted us, if that sight had not been so horrific. Rivers was kneeling next to a metal cage of the type used to contain large animals. There were about a dozen such cages in this area, but only two were occupied. Olo and Antonio were lying on their sides. They were naked, and covered in their own excrement. Both were semiconscious and in obvious pain.

Rivers appeared to be evaluating Olo's condition without touching him. He jumped when he was poked in the back by Sergeant Reyes' rifle. He stumbled to his feet and began to speak. Then he looked around and seemed to realise that nothing he could say could mitigate, or explain, his situation. In desperation, he reached inside of his hospital gown and attempted to remove a small pistol. It had not quite cleared his cumbersome outer garment when Sergeant Cruz applied the butt of his rifle to Rivers' forehead. The dog man crashed against Olo's cage, unconscious.

Now our attention shifted to the two unfortunate Igorots. Olo was groaning and attempting to communicate with us. Cruz leaned over and opened his kennel. I did the same for Antonio, but when he did not move I confirmed that he was already dead.

Olo had enough energy to crawl out of his cage. He climbed over Rivers' unconscious body, and before any of us could intervene, he removed the revolver from Rivers' hand, placed it under his captor's chin, and fired.

Holmes was the first to speak. "So much for our plan to press the dog man for information." None of us could blame Olo for his action, however.

Nor could we do much to alleviate his suffering. We provided him with water from the office, which he drank ferociously. Then I dampened two pieces of cloth and applied them as compresses to his forehead, which seemed to relieve their pain a bit. After some time Olo attempted to speak. Reyes translated the Igorot's words. "He thanks us for our help, but now he asks that we shoot him to end his suffering."

I asked Reyes to tell the Igorot that I was a doctor and that I would provide him with medicine. Then I informed Holmes and Loving that Sergeant Cruz and I should take the barouche back to town and find a druggist. When no one protested we returned to the small office, removed our protective gear and rushed out of the warehouse.

We fast-walked the mile back to our carriage and both of us climbed up in the driver's seat. Cruz pushed our horse and we made good time into town. We found a chemist and I presented my credentials as a physician. I requested morphine, and a hypodermic needle. When the pharmacist heard my request he looked suspicious. "I don't think I can fill that prescription for a person who does not have an American medical degree." At which point, Cruz stepped forward and unslung his rifle. This ended the discussion.

Cruz once again pressed our horse to the limit and we were soon back at the warehouse. Our group had moved to the small office and removed their protective garments. I could tell by the expression on my friend's face that we were too late. "Olo passed away a few minutes after you left, Watson." I resisted asking the obvious question: Had he been helped on his way?

Holmes then stated, "He was able to provide a bit more information before he died. He said that they had been overpowered by three men when they left the fairgrounds with the dog man. They were injected with a powerful drug and woke up in these cages, naked. Olo said that when he first awoke he saw the three men, in full protective garb, carrying five or six dead bodies out of the warehouse. He noted that one of these corpses was Japanese."

"This does not give us much to go on, Holmes."

"The information is sparse, but not without value, Watson. For instance, we know that these two unfortunate individuals were brought here so that they could be subjected to some form of fast acting and quite virulent disease, for reasons that we cannot, at this point, surmise. We can also be confident that a number of Asians suffered the same fate as our two Igorots. We also know that the three men who were removing the dead bodies must have used a wagon to transport them. Finally, and most importantly, since we know that the dog man came here on foot we can safely assume that he did not come here to transport the bodies. He came here to monitor the progress of Olo and Antonio's illness and to await the return of his co-conspirators with the wagon."

"Then our next steps are clear, Holmes. We hide our barouche and position ourselves outside of the warehouse to await the arrival of these villains. We capture them and compel them to tell us their plans."

"Well done, Watson, but I might recommend one variation in your strategy." Holmes explained his idea and we all concurred, albeit grudgingly.

Twenty-Five

The next three hours passed very slowly. Holmes had proposed that we don our protective gear once again and remain in the small office until the arrival of the wagon. The fact that the two windows were open in the office made the situation tolerable, if not pleasant. When the wagon finally arrived the three men came into the office to dress in their masks, gloves and gowns. The look of shock on their faces when they confronted our band, armed with rifles and pistols, confirmed the wisdom of Sherlock's recommendation. Cruz handed his rifle to Holmes and approached the three criminals. He searched each man and removed various weapons and their wallets — which provided us with their names. Then all three were paraded out of the office and into the back of the warehouse. They gasped when they saw the two Igorots outside of their cages and the body of Rivers lying next to Olo. All three stopped and began to back up until they were prodded by our weapons.

"Gentlemen," Holmes stated, "I am going to ask you some questions. Every time that I am not satisfied with your answers my colleague will push you one step closer to the corpses with his rifle. At a certain point, if we are still not content with your answers we will place all of you in that cage..." Holmes pointed to the one metal cage that was much bigger than the rest. "In the company of our two deceased Filipinos. We will leave you there with an armed guard while we return to Saint Louis to report to the police."

The three men were terrified, but their first instincts were to feign ignorance. The one whose name was Harrison spoke first. "We don't know anything about corpses. We were hired simply to deliver the wagon and then make our way back to town on foot." Holmes nodded to Sergeant Reyes, who pushed Harrison a step closer to the dead bodies. The man was on the verge of fainting. "All right, we were paid to deliver these two bodies to a small shed on the edge of the Philippine Compound."

"Is this the same place where you delivered the other bodies?" Harrison nodded. "And how many bodies are already stored at this location?"

Harrison looked at his partners and then stammered, "Twelve."

"So with these two unfortunates we have a total of fourteen victims. But why were they killed, and why in this manner?"

"We don't know anything about that." Another prod from Reyes. A shriek of fear from Harrison. "All we know is that we were told by Rivers to meet him here and to help him to deliver these two late tonight and then we would be needed to move all of the bodies to a different location within the Philippine Compound. We were not told where precisely. Rivers said that he would tell us the location when we needed to know. Really, that is all we know."

Holmes continued: "Now, what can any of you tell us about the disease that killed these two?"

"We weren't told anything, except that we needed to wear the protective costumes whenever we were near the Asians."

"That is unfortunate. Sergeant Reyes…"

Bracing for another prod, Harrison said, "No, honest!" then he looked down at Olo's body. "I do remember hearing Rivers talking to one of the Filipinos. He was in his cage and Rivers was poking him with a stick and laughing. He said, 'You should be honoured. We gave you a dose of something fit for an emperor'. I don't know what Rivers meant by that."

I was startled by this comment. I began to speak but then decided to hold my tongue until I had confirmed my worst suspicions.

Holmes reached into his jacket and removed his map of the fairgrounds. He handed Harrison a pencil and instructed him to mark the precise location of the shed that was being used to store the bodies. Harrison looked closely at the map and then made his mark on a section of the grounds that was in the northeast part of the Philippine Compound.

At this point, Holmes had concluded that we had extracted all the useful information from our three villains. We marched them back into the office, removed their belts and used them to tie their hands behind their backs. They were placed on the floor and Sergeant Cruz was given guard duty. It was not clear if Holmes was sincere when he told Cruz, "Shoot any of these individuals if they make a move, or if you just feel the inclination to exterminate these vermin. We will send the police to take charge of this situation and relieve you." We then removed our protective clothing but carried them with us to the barouche. Before reporting to the police we went to the fairgrounds and were fortunate to find Rhymes still at his office. We gave him an edited account of our adventure — he was appropriately shocked but quickly gained control. He telephoned the chief of the Saint Louis Police and arranged for a meeting. I was reassured by the tone of their conversation — indicative of both familiarity and mutual respect. I could only imagine how our party — two Brits, a Filipino and an American Negro — would have been treated if we had arrived at the police station without Rhymes, rattling on about multiple murders and naked prisoners in dog cages.

The chief of police, whose name was Golding, sent two of his officers to relieve Cruz and collect the three prisoners at the warehouse. Our group, now expanded to include a number of police officers, loaded into our carriage and two police automobiles and proceeded to the area that Harrison had identified on the map. When we arrived we positioned ourselves near the shed but did not immediately attempt to enter. After some minutes with no apparent activity the chief instructed two of his armed men to approach the shed. They drew their weapons, and one man lit a lantern, and they began to move cautiously toward the small building. I stopped them immediately and handed them the small jar of menthol which I had taken from the warehouse. I instructed them on how to use the ointment and also advised them to tie handkerchiefs around their faces, as masks. "And don't go inside of the building. Just confirm that there is no resistance from inside and then remain at the door and use your lantern." Both men looked at their superior to get confirmation, and were rewarded by a nod from the chief.

The door was locked, but it opened easily when one of the officers put his shoulder to it. As soon as the door gave way, the dreadful odour that we had confronted at the warehouse struck us. Both of the officers began to gag, and then one passed out. We dragged him back and after he was revived, the police chief looked into the shed and then quickly stepped back. "What possible reason would any person or group have for perpetrating this... horror?"

"All that we know at this point," said Holmes, "is that the bodies were to be transported to another location within the Philippine Compound."

I responded, "Perhaps the bodies can tell us a bit more." I returned to our carriage and once again donned the entire protective costume. After adding another dose of menthol I commandeered the lantern from the policeman and walked slowly to the entrance of the shed.

The victims were stacked one upon the other, making two piles that reached to my waist. I approached the bodies and shone the light on the person on top of one of the piles. He was a man of approximately thirty years of age, lying on his stomach. I turned him over and began to examine him. It took no time to discover precisely what I feared. The dead man exhibited buboes, some of which exuded pus, in his groin area and armpits. I also noted signs of necrosis on his hands and nose. I went outside and removed all of my protective gear. I threw it on the ground and stated, "This should all be burned, along with the rest of the protective material that we brought from the warehouse. In fact, after we bury the victims and remove the vials that are stored in the small office at the warehouse the authorities should probably burn both this shed and the warehouse."

I approached my companions and noticed that they all (including Sherlock!) took a step back. "Gentlemen, I am reasonably confident that these poor individuals died from some form of plague, specifically a version of Bacterium Pestis. The first known case of this epidemic is named after the Roman emperor, Justinian, who ruled during the sixth century, when the epidemic raged over much of the eastern Mediterranean. Some historians claim that he was one of the lucky ones, in that he contracted the disease but survived it. One fourth of the population was not so fortunate."

I allowed my words to sink in before continuing. "The body that I just examined shows some of the classic symptoms of this disease. In Justinian's time the plague was spread by fleas and rats, but over the centuries different forms of Bacterium Pestis have surfaced. My guess is that we are not looking at a flea-born epidemic, because if that were the case we would have found evidence of the cultivation and use of the insects at the warehouse. I suspect that these Filipinos died from a form of the plague that is spread by human contact and perhaps by airborne particles... which makes it especially dangerous."

As I was speaking, I noticed that all the members of our group were hanging on my words, and that I had become the person in charge. My training as a physician, and in particular my experience as a field surgeon in Afghanistan, had prepared me for this role, and my colleagues needed no convincing. Not even Holmes. My friend knew a great deal about poisons and their effects on the body, but aside from that topic he had only a very superficial knowledge of medicine. Indeed, there had been occasions in the past when I had tried to instruct him on medical matters and he had rejected my efforts. Holmes explained this behaviour during the case that I called The Five Orange Pips:

'A man should keep his little brain-attic stocked
with all the furniture that he is likely to use, and
the rest he can put away in the lumber-room of
his library, where he can get it if he wants it.'

Holmes knew that I was always available if he needed to 'get' medical information. And I realised that this information had never been more important than at this moment.

My first instructions were to Chief Golding. "Please send a contingent of police officers to the warehouse and also increase the number of officers here at the shed. Instruct them to establish a secure perimeter around both buildings, but not to enter. Then I would appreciate it if you would accompany me to the Washington University School of Medicine so that we can recruit help with the disposal of the bodies and the testing of the vials of clear liquid that were stored in the cabinet at the warehouse. Hopefully they will find both samples of the plague and vaccines for its suppression."

"Sherlock, I would recommend that you, Mr Rhymes and Lieutenant Loving attempt to get a few hours of sleep, so that you will be ready for tomorrow. I suspect that things will come to a head very soon after the people in charge of this plot discover that their plans are unravelling."

Rhymes recommended that he and Holmes take the barouche to the Inside Inn. Holmes agreed, and the two men departed. I asked Lieutenant Loving if he needed transport to his room in the Philippine Compound. He assured me that it was a short walk, and he left, after congratulating Sergeant Reyes for his exemplary service. I reminded him that Sergeant Cruz was also deserving of special recognition.

Over the next few hours Golding and I arranged for the police to secure the two locations and then made our way to the hospital with a small contingent of officers. By this time it was late at night, so that we were greeted by a small group of nurses and doctors. Golding took charge. He obtained the names and addresses of the doctors and administrators who were in charge of the facility and then sent his officers to those addresses to roust the sleeping individuals. By two in the morning we had convened the leadership of the hospital, and after we had explained the situation, they began to issue instructions and make preparations. I was impressed with their efficiency, and very pleased to discover that the hospital had a research laboratory on site. I was introduced to the director of this facility, Doctor Albert Woodruff, who demonstrated a familiarity with the recent work of a French physician named Alexandre Yersin, whose research with plague victims in Hong Kong was generating international attention.

Once the arrangements were in place I asked if there was a doctor's lounge where I could rest for a few hours. I said goodbye to Golding and we agreed to meet at the hospital at nine in the morning.

Twenty-Six

I awoke the next morning to the sound of thunder and the pelting of heavy rain. I would later discover that this was a very fortuitous development.

After a quick breakfast I met with Dr Woodruff in his laboratory. He reported that he had made some very preliminary tests of the vials of clear liquid that had been brought from the warehouse. "I am inclined to agree with you that this strain of Bacterium Pestis is probably spread by human-to-human contact and by airborne transmission."

"Then we are looking at a form of pneumonic plague," I stated, "similar to the 'black death' in fourteenth century Europe."

"That is correct, although I cannot, for the life of me, understand why anyone would be motivated to unleash such a disease on America in the twentieth century."

Woodruff informed me that he had already reached out, by telephone and telegram, to the nation's leading experts on epidemics. "Some are already on their way here to assist us, and some have requested samples so that they can examine the plague in their own laboratories. I hope that this proves to be unnecessary, but we have to be especially cautious here in Saint Louis. As you may know, Doctor, we had a very unfortunate incident just three years ago, when our Municipal Health Authority began inoculating children for Diphtheria. They were using an antitoxin from a horse, which turned out to be contaminated with tetanus. Thirteen children died as a result. So we cannot be too cautious about this particular virus. If it does transpire that we need to vaccinate the public to protect them against this pathogen, I will need all of the authoritative scientific support that I can muster to convince the local population that they can trust the vaccine."

I was encouraged by Woodruff's preparations, and I thanked him for his efforts. We agreed to meet later in the day to assess the progress that he and his team had made. By this time it was nine in the morning and Golding was waiting for me in the entrance to the hospital. He was accompanied by an armed officer and a driver, who ushered us into a landau. We left immediately for the Inside Inn, where we were joined by Holmes, Loving and Rhymes. Golding went to the reception desk and requested a meeting room. After we were settled in, the concierge brought us an assortment of pastries, fruit, coffee and (an accommodation to the British accents that he heard) scones and tea.

Holmes took charge. "Gentlemen, let us begin by asking ourselves if our interventions last night have put an end to the threat? Are we now safe?"

Loving was the first to respond. "To answer that question we must first ask what could possibly have been accomplished by the placement of fourteen plague-infected bodies in the Philippine Compound. Were they meant to infect the Filipino natives?"

"Under normal circumstances," I noted, "the corpses of pneumonic plague victims would not be infectious. The hideously damaged bodies would have shocked those natives that saw them, and the discovery of the bodies would have generated hysterical commentary in the local press. It is conceivable that the Philippine Compound might have been closed by the administrators of the fair, and all of the natives might have been sent back to their homes. But what would have been accomplished?"

Loving spoke once again. "We also need to remind ourselves that some of the victims were Japanese and Chinese."

"Quite so, Lieutenant," Holmes replied. "These outcomes do not seem to justify the obvious effort that went into this crime. So we must consider the very real likelihood that we have only interrupted the first stage in a more ambitious scheme. Let us assume that the bodies were supposed to be discovered by Filipino natives and fairgoers. Now let us also assume that these discoveries were meant to generate widespread fear, speculation, rumours. I put it to you that all of this was meant to serve as a preface for some more outrageous act... Watson, you stated that this form of the plague could be spread by human contact or by airborne transmission. Of those two modes of transmission, the latter would surely be more potentially destructive, if it could be accomplished. But how? Perhaps we need to rely upon some experts."

Holmes explained what he was thinking and our group prepared to disband. Fortunately, the concierge appeared with umbrellas to protect us against the heavy rain. Golding went back to police headquarters to prepare for population control in the event of the spread of the disease. Rhymes and Loving joined Holmes and me in a waiting four-wheeler. Holmes instructed the driver to take us to the concourse. We travelled to the eastern end of the fairgrounds and our driver deposited us in front of a large building with an open front. Two men were inside, working on a flying machine. They grabbed two umbrellas and came out to greet us. Wilbur Wright sported an impressive moustache. His brother Orville was clean shaven, taller, with piercing eyes and a sharply protruding chin. I was struck by how much this second brother resembled Holmes. The brothers knew Smythe, who shook their hands and then introduced them to Loving, Holmes and me. My friend could not disguise his excitement at meeting the aeronauts. As we walked into their hangar Holmes stated, "It is an honour to meet you, gentlemen. I have followed your efforts to conquer gravity. And this..." he pointed to the machine inside of the building. "Must be the famous *Flyer II*."

The brothers were quick to return the compliment. Wilbur assured my friend that they were very familiar with his exploits. "And Doctor Watson, of course, who has provided such dramatic accounts of these adventures. To what do we owe the honour of your visit?"

"We are here to draw upon your expertise regarding various modes of aerial transport."

The brothers led us further into their shelter, where they had a long drafting table and a few chairs. I knew that my friend would have preferred to stay in the front of the shed so that he could have inspected the flying machine, but he realised that he had other priorities. He did, however, touch the lower wing on the Flyer II as we walked past it.

"Gentlemen, in confidence, we suspect that someone is plotting to attack the fair with an airborne virus. If we are correct, then we must assume that this person intends to use some form of airship to transmit the disease. We would be most grateful for your insights about the type of flying machine that would be needed to accomplish this task."

The brothers were visibly shocked by my friend's comments. After a few moments thought, Orville spoke. "As you probably know, Mr Holmes, the fair attracted many aviators with its offer of a hundred-thousand-dollar prize for the winner of the aerial concourse. Most of the aircraft that are still here are dirigibles, which rely on lighter-than-air hydrogen gas to go aloft. There are also gliders, hot air balloons, and a couple of aircraft like ours. We came to Saint Louis to compete in the concourse, but once we were here it became obvious that the rules of the competition favoured dirigibles, so we decided not to participate. We chose to remain here, however, to enjoy the fair and to interact with our competitors and our partners in the aeronautic field. These months have given us an opportunity to evaluate all of the different forms of air travel at the fair. Based on that experience, I would say that a dirigible would be the best means of delivering a toxic gas over a wide area. Dirigibles are big enough to carry the necessary equipment and manoeuvrable enough to allow the pilot to steer the aircraft over the target area. Would you agree, Wilbur? His brother nodded his head.

"And which of the competing dirigibles would be the most capable of accomplishing this feat?"

Wilbur was quick to answer. "If you had asked us a few months ago, I am sure that we would have agreed that Alberto Santos-Dumont's airship would have been the obvious candidate. It was universally recognised as the likely winner of the prize, until the accident."

"No accident, brother" Orville intervened. "The dirigible was destroyed — with long deep slashes by a knife when the night watchman left his post and went for coffee. Santos-Dumont went right back home to Paris. No one was arrested for the crime."

"And who stood to gain the most from this act of vandalism?"

"Several aeronauts had a fair shot at the prize with Santos-Dumont out of the way: The German Count von Zeppelin, Captain Tom Baldwin with his *California Arrow*... And I guess you could say that the fellow from

New York benefitted, although he never did compete for the prize."

Wilbur explained. "My brother is referring to an amateur who was allowed to enter the competition as the substitute for Santos-Dumont after the incident, a retired military man by the name of Smythe. He has a dirigible named *Victoria* which he takes over the fairgrounds from time to time. Perhaps you have seen it."

Holmes and I looked at each other. "That cannot be a coincidence, Holmes. When we met the general in New York I remember informing him that we were on our way to the World's Fair, but he said nothing about being in Saint Louis."

I felt the need to be certain, however. "Are you referring to General Allen Smythe, an older gentleman with a decided limp?"

"Yes, precisely."

"Would you happen to know where General Smythe keeps his dirigible?"

The brothers conversed for a couple of minutes and then directed us to a location in the southeast portion of the fairgrounds. Our driver said that he knew the area. We thanked the aeronauts and immediately departed.

Twenty-Seven

Our driver deposited us some distance from the hangar that housed the *Victoria*. We positioned ourselves under a large tree, which provided partial protection from the rain. From this vantage point we had a clear view of Smythe's hangar, but we saw no movement outside of the structure for about an hour, until the rain stopped. I suddenly realised that if Smythe was indeed intent on attacking the fair with an airborne plague he would not have been able to dispense it until the rain stopped. I also realised that now that the sun had returned guests would be flooding back into the fairgrounds — providing Smythe with a rich pool of targets.

As if in response to my musings, the large door in the front of the hangar opened and six men began to pull a dirigible out on a wheeled platform and prepare it for flight. The *Victoria* was relatively small, compared to Count von Zeppelin's airship that had passed over our heads the other day. It was oval shaped, like a rugby ball. We saw Smythe standing near the cabin of the dirigible, giving instructions to his assistants.

Holmes was silent for a few moments. "I think that we have arrived just in time, Watson. If I am not mistaken,

General Smythe intends to use the airship to disseminate the airborne virus."

Loving reached for his service pistol and said, "We should stop them before they can launch."

Holmes responded, "I understand your concern, Lieutenant, but you will note that four of the workers have rifles strapped across their backs and we can assume that the others have pistols. The rifles would give them a significant advantage as soon as they saw us approaching. There may also be more men in the hangar."

Holmes then pulled out his map of the fairgrounds and after tracing a path across the centre of the map he leaned forward and gave me my instructions. My first reaction was to refuse, but then Holmes asked me, "Do you see any other way to protect the lives of hundreds, or perhaps thousands, of innocent people?" My silence conveyed my grudging assent.

Holmes then said, "One more thing, Watson." He reached into his coat and withdrew the pistol that he had taken from the dead Secret Service agent and inspected it. "This weapon has only four shots. Since Lieutenant Loving is armed with his service revolver I think it would be best if you gave me your gun." He placed one weapon in each pocket of his mackintosh and we all climbed back in the cab.

Holmes told our driver to return at top speed to the centre of the fair. When we arrived Loving and I exited the cab and Holmes and Rhymes continued on. Loving and I walked at a brisk pace to our destination, while I used this opportunity to explain the plan to the lieutenant.

Loving and I arrived at our destination at about the same time that Holmes and Rhymes reached theirs. I shook hands with Padre Himalaya, and before he could ask me the reason for my visit I spoke. "Father, would you happen to have a pair of binoculars that I might borrow?" He confirmed that he did have a pair and went into his office to collect them. When he returned, I gave them to Loving, who directed them toward the centre of the fairgrounds. "They are there."

Padre Himalaya could not restrain himself. "What is it that you gentlemen are doing, and who are you looking at with the glasses?"

I decided that there was no value in trying to explain. "Father, with sincere apologies, my colleague and I must escort you inside your laboratory and make certain that you cannot interfere with our activities." The priest began to sputter a complaint, but he was quickly silenced by Loving, who had unholstered his Colt. We led him inside and instructed him to be seated. We then found enough rope to tie both his hands and his feet. "We will be back to untie you as soon as it is practicable, and we would ask you not to call for help or make a ruckus. Otherwise we will have to silence you." I left that last statement hanging in the air to encourage him to use his imagination. I also reassured myself that I was actually doing the priest a favour by making him a prisoner, since no matter what transpired he could not be accused, or accuse himself, of being complicit.

Once outside Loving handed me the binoculars and I trained them on the Great Wheel. It was stopped, and I was able to confirm that none of the gondolas were occupied except for the highest one. "Rhymes has succeeded in convincing the operator to empty all of the gondolas save one." I could see Holmes inside the gondola at the top of the wheel, and I noticed that the door was open. As I watched, Holmes began to climb out of the cabin and onto its roof. I held my breath as he pulled himself up with great effort. At one point, the door that was swinging freely in the wind slammed into his back, but he did not lose his grip. I was reminded that neither Holmes nor I were young.

When my friend finally made it to the roof he stretched out on his stomach to gain his sense of balance. Then he began to slowly stand up with his feet far apart and his hands outstretched. I followed his gaze in the direction from which we had come. In the distance I could see a dirigible moving slowly in our general direction.

It was time for me to play my part. Loving and I looked at the massive Pyreliophorus. I was glad that I had paid attention when Padre Himalaya demonstrated the device. I pulled the lever that turned the machine on, and I began to rotate it so that it was aimed toward the sky. Then I had to make adjustments in the mirrors which coated the inside of the device, so that it was aimed at a focal point approximately one hundred meters over our heads. I threw the switch that uncovered the back of the machine, so that it would allow sunlight in to generate heat. And nothing happened…

"Damn, what did I do wrong?" I was about to ask Loving to bring the priest outside and force him at gunpoint to make the necessary adjustments, when the lieutenant guided my attention upward, to a single puffy cloud that was blocking out the sun.

I realised that there was nothing to be done but wait patiently for the cloud to pass. Now I could hear the sound of the motor that propelled the dirigible as it approached overhead. I raised the binoculars and saw my friend, still balancing on the roof of the gondola as the airship approached. I thought of asking the priest to offer an intercessory prayer to move the cloud, but a rejected this idea as blasphemous in light of what I intended to do. So we waited, as the dirigible passed over our heads, dangling its two long tether ropes. I could see one man at the controls of the airship, inside of a small cabin attached to the underside of the dirigible.

And suddenly, the cloud began to move… and the sun began to focus its power through the lens of the Pyreliophorus. I made some adjustments that allowed me to aim the device at the rear of the dirigible, which by this time was approaching the Great Wheel. I realised that what I was about to do would place my friend in mortal danger, but I knew for certain that he was prepared to accept this risk.

Then I flipped the switch that sent a blinding beam of light directly at the dirigible. We could see that the beam had reached its target, but we were not rewarded with the expected explosion. Loving spoke, "The beam is not strong enough to penetrate a moving target."

By this time the airship was quite close to Holmes' location, and he could see the problem. As I watched through the binoculars, my friend backed up to the edge of the roof and then ran across the top of the gondola and launched himself at the airship. At first I thought that he was trying to reach the cabin that held the pilot of the airship. I gasped, and shouted, "Holmes!" when it appeared that my friend had missed his target. I fell to my knees in shock and dropped the field glasses, believing that I had just seen my friend fall to his death.

Then Loving put his hand on my shoulder and pointed at the dirigible. "Look." Holmes was holding onto the long tether which hung from the cabin. He lowered himself down on the rope and then began to swing toward the wheel, which was now at its closest point with the *Victoria*. After three long arcs his feet touched the top of the gondola. He pushed off and then, with one final swing he landed back on the roof, still holding onto the tether. As soon as he landed Holmes scrambled to run the rope through some of the metal braces that held the wheel together.

Almost immediately, the Great Wheel began to groan with the sound of bending metal, and the *Victoria* stopped moving. I saw my opportunity to focus the beam of the Pyreliophorus on a single point at the back of the dirigible. Then I regained the field glasses. I could see that the beam was still somewhat dispersed, but with the dirigible anchored in place by the tether line it was beginning to have its effect.

Then I saw through the binoculars that the pilot was running to the back of the cabin. He grabbed a fire axe off of the wall and raised it over his head. I realised that he was about to cut the tether rope. But before he could act, I saw Holmes, who was lying on his stomach on the roof of the cabin, fire four shots from my revolver. The pilot fell. Holmes then ran to the edge of the gondola and climbed onto the metalwork of the wheel. He began to quickly lower himself down, and he had reached the hub of the wheel when the dirigible exploded. I could feel the heat on my face although we were more than a hundred and fifty meters away. Fairgoers ran screaming in all directions as the remains of the airship fell from the sky.

Loving and I wasted no time. We untied Padre Himalaya, who was sputtering with rage. I apologised once again, and assured him that someone would explain what had transpired, and why. Then we made our way on foot to the Great Wheel. The remains of the *Victoria* were still hanging from it by the tether rope.

We found Holmes and Rhymes sitting on a bench. My friend's jacket was on the ground, still smouldering. "I was fortunate, Watson. The gondola took the brunt of the explosion. I was able to climb down from the wheel, with some difficulty."

Holmes did not look fortunate. He was suffering from minor burns to the backs of his hands, as well as his back and neck area. The hair on the back of his head was singed. His palms were also badly scraped from his rapid descent on the wheel.

Rhymes had already taken charge, assisting the injured and reassuring the public. He sent for Golding, who arrived with a substantial contingent of officers to cordon off the area. Rhymes also commandeered a number of automobiles, and instructed the drivers to take the wounded to the hospital. Fortunately, there were no fatalities except for the pilot of the dirigible. I asked Rhymes to arrange for me to take Holmes to the hospital. My friend began to speak, no doubt to assure me that he did not need medical treatment. But he was simply too exhausted to spar with me.

When we arrived at the hospital I met with Dr Woodruff and informed him of what had taken place at the fair. He advised me that the hospital was coping with about a dozen injuries, which ranged from superficial to serious. It struck me that this was the best that could have been hoped for, in light of the huge crowd at the fair that day. Woodruff also offered to send a team to inspect the area around the wheel, to confirm that there were no residual strains of the virus.

While he was being treated for burns and scrapes, Holmes said, "This was a near-run thing, Watson. My actions were guided by four assumptions, any one of which could have been incorrect. First, I supposed that Smythe's target was the Philippine Compound, since the majority of the infected victims were Filipino. But this supposition required us to discount the fact that there were also Japanese and Chinese among the victims. Second, I based my plan on a belief that the airship would take the most direct route from its hangar to the Philippine Compound, so that it would pass very close to both the Great Wheel and the Pyreliophorus. Third, I gambled that the dirigible would fly slowly and not too high above the ground, to avoid the dispersal of the airborne virus before it reached its targets. I assumed that this would make the airship vulnerable to destruction by the Pyreliophorus. I positioned myself on top of the Great Wheel as a fallback in the event that you were not able to destroy the dirigible with the sun machine. I was prepared to use my two pistols on the gas bag if necessary, but I did not hold out much hope that this would be sufficient to ignite the hydrogen. Finally, my plan was based upon an article of faith — that a massive explosion, triggered by the intense heat of the Pyreliophorus would completely destroy the virus." Holmes paused for a moment and then said, "I am sure that you know me well enough, Watson, to understand how uncomfortable I am with any assumption that is not based on solid evidence. And I expect that we will have to wait quite a while to be certain that the plague has been completely destroyed."

I discussed this last issue with Dr Woodruff later that day, and I was reassured by the efforts that he had taken to secure the area near the wheel and to establish guidelines for testing those fairgoers who had been close to the explosion. Woodruff also pleased Holmes by informing him that he could return to his hotel as soon as his injuries had been taken care of.

By the time that we arrived back at the hotel it was too late for dinner. We were both quite hungry, however, so we asked a bellman if it would be possible to get anything to eat. He disappeared into the kitchen and returned a few minutes later to inform us, "The chef is preparing hot dogs for each of you, with sauerkraut." He recommended Schlitz Beer to accompany the hot dogs. We were too tired to reject his advice. When the hot dogs arrived we both added yellow mustard and quickly dispensed with them. The beer, as we expected, was too cold and too thin, but the waiter had been correct. It was a good companion to our hot dogs.

"I am looking forward to a good night's sleep, Holmes. Then tomorrow we will need to meet with Golding, Loving and Rhymes to discuss next steps."

"Quite so, Watson. We can be very pleased with the results of our efforts today. But there are still many questions to be answered. Most notably, why would Smythe wish to unleash a plague on unsuspecting fairgoers? We cannot feel safe until we know the answer to that question."

Twenty-Eight

Our group met at police headquarters the next day. Holmes began the discussion with the question that he had asked me the night before. "Why would Smythe — why would anyone — release a plague? And why would anyone do so at a World's Fair, with thousands of potential victims returning home to virtually every state in the United States, and many foreign countries?"

Loving volunteered that perhaps it was as simple as lunacy. I responded that Holmes and I had spent an evening with Smythe and he did not strike me as a deranged person. Holmes added that most lunatics were solitary individuals, and it was hard to imagine this ambitious scheme — involving the production of a large quantity of plague virus, the kidnapping of more than a dozen individuals, and the use of a dirigible — to be engineered by one man.

Rhymes picked up the discussion. "So we are looking for a criminal conspiracy with considerable scientific and financial resources."

"I am afraid so," stated Holmes. "This makes our job easier in one sense. It narrows the field to big, powerful actors."

Loving nodded, "But it means that we will have to include in our list of possible culprits agents of foreign governments who would have the resources necessary to engage in this type of mass destruction."

Holmes and I looked at each other but remained silent. My friend and I had given our word to Mycroft that we would not discuss with outsiders our adventure with the Russians. Furthermore, I had great difficulty imagining the czar initiating a plague in the United States. It would trigger an all-out war if the plot was exposed, at a time when neither Moscow nor the other major international actors were prepared for war. Holmes stated, "I know someone who can assist us in determining whether a foreign government is involved. In the meantime I recommend that we focus on other candidates."

The discussion continued for about an hour, at which time Loving brought us back to the fundamental question: "What could this man Smythe have hoped to accomplish by killing Asians?"

I decided to share with the group a theory that I had been developing since we discovered the Filipino victims in the warehouse. "It is possible that Smythe's intention was to convince the American public that Asians in general, and the Filipinos in particular, had brought the epidemic to the fair and that from there Smythe expected the plague to travel across the country, spreading panic and turning public opinion against the Open Door strategy."

My statement was met with silence around the table, until Holmes said, "Whatever motive there was for

Smythe's actions, we are not likely to discover it here in Saint Louis." Then he informed the group of the plans that he and I had agreed upon that morning. "Dr Watson and I will be taking the three p.m. train back to New York City today. That is where Smythe lived, and it is where he served as president of something called the Anglo-Saxon Club, so it seems like the most propitious location for the next stage in our investigation. I encourage all of you to continue your inquiries here in Saint Louis. We can be reached in New York at the Algonquin Hotel."

Holmes had sent a telegram to Hastings that morning, informing him of our plans, and before we checked out of our hotel the concierge informed us that Hastings had booked our overnight train reservations, made our dinner reservations in the dining car, and reserved our rooms in the Algonquin in New York.

I was beginning to lose count of the number of times we had used the overnight train which connected Saint Louis with the East Coast. The only consolation was that we had learned the names of our sleeping car porter and our waiter, and both were exceedingly friendly and attentive.

We lingered over the meal and the after-dinner liquors. When we were finished, and most of the guests had retired, Holmes packed his clay pipe and lit it carefully. "Watson, I am anxious to move forward with our inquiries in New York. I hope that we are not on a fool's errand in that city." After a few minutes of silence my friend said, "When we get to our hotel I will send a telegram to Mycroft to inform him of our recent activities and to solicit his opinion on the possibility that a government is behind the attack at the fair. I will also send a telegram to Golding to confirm that he has succeeded in arresting Smythe's assistants. It is possible that some of these individuals had no knowledge of what the general was doing, but this will be for the Saint Louis Police to sort out. Finally, I will send a third telegram to Dr Woodruff in Saint Louis, to confirm one fact. After I have sent these messages I would propose that we visit Detective Inspector Abrams to recruit his help while we are in New York." I concurred with Holmes' plans, and ordered a second Armagnac.

Twenty-Nine

Hastings was waiting for us when we exited the train in New York. He was anxious to hear about our adventures at the fair, and I gave him a brief accounting. When I was finished, he turned to Holmes and asked, "And did you actually kill Smythe with your pistol?"

I answered for my friend. "You can understand that it was very difficult to inspect the body of General Smythe after the conflagration. It was badly burned and required considerable… reassembly. Even if the general did survive Holmes' bullets, he certainly did not survive for long."

We were welcomed back to the Algonquin hotel by the general manager. He informed us that we had been upgraded to adjoining suites on the top floor of the hotel. He escorted us to our rooms, which were quite spacious. "The hotel was originally designed for long term lease occupants, which explains the size of your rooms. But it soon became clear that it would be more profitable to convert it into a hotel." We interrupted him in full flow and thanked him profusely. Then Holmes edged him out of the room.

One hour later we were down at the reception desk, where Holmes constructed his three telegrams. He then used the hotel phone to contact Inspector Abrams and ask if we could meet with him. Abrams agreed immediately and offered to join us in the lobby of the Algonquin. He arrived an hour later with a driver and one patrolman. We settled around a corner table and requested tea. Holmes did most of the talking but he was kind enough to give me credit for identifying the threat and taking the necessary steps to contain it. "We could not have succeeded in Watson's absence."

When Holmes had finished, Abrams asked, "If the threat has been destroyed, why are you continuing your investigations here in New York?"

"Because it stretches credulity to assume that General Smythe acted alone. And since the general lived and worked in this city it seems reasonable to begin our search for his collaborators here. Which brings me to a request, Inspector: Dr Watson and I intend to pay a visit to the Anglo-Saxon Club tomorrow, and it would be very beneficial if you could help us to prepare for this visit with information regarding the individuals who are in charge of that club, including information about their finances."

Abrams assured us that he would be happy to look into the individuals associated with the Anglo-Saxon Club, including General Smythe. We thanked him and said our goodbyes.

Holmes and I remained at the hotel for the rest of the afternoon, tying up loose ends. Holmes read a message from Mycroft which was delivered by a member of the British Embassy staff. It employed the same Fibonacci code that he had employed in Saint Louis. "Watson, I must recommend to my brother that he employ greater originality in his encoded communications." The concierge provided my friend with a pen and a piece of stationary and in a few minutes Holmes had deciphered the message. As we had expected, Mycroft confirmed that the attack on the World's Fair was probably not done by a foreign government.

Holmes then telephoned the Anglo-Saxon Club and made arrangements for a visit the next afternoon. Our pretext was that we had spent time with General Smythe at the fair and wished to report on his last days.

While my friend busied himself with these arrangements I telephoned Mr and Mrs Norton and invited them to dinner. I was very pleased by their enthusiastic acceptance.

We met our friends at Sherry's restaurant, recommended by our concierge both for its haute cuisine and because of its proximity to our hotel. We benefitted from Irene's presence. She was immediately recognised by the maître d', who escorted us to a table while lavishing praise on her. "I had the good fortune to see you in Traviata recently…" He attracted our waiter and instructed him to provide us with champagne while we perused the menu.

Godfrey patted his wife's hand and said, "I commend him for his good taste. Irene's Violetta is among her best roles. By now, of course, she can perform it in her sleep."

Irene laughed and admitted, that "the Metropolitan Opera had beaten poor Violetta to death over the years."

Then she attempted to move the conversation in a different direction. "This restaurant is well known for its ambitious American menu, but it is also notorious for the events that have taken place here. Last year it served a meal for thirty-six guests, all of whom were on horseback. The food was placed on trays attached to the saddles, and each guest had a saddlebag full of iced champagne, which they drank through a rubber tube. The meal actually took place on the fourth floor of the restaurant," she pointed upward, "with horses and riders transported up and down by a freight elevator. Each guest paid two hundred and fifty dollars for the privilege…"

Godfrey picked up the thread. "And they wonder why so many Europeans make fun of American society…"

I responded, "Speaking only for Britain, we have no shortage of our own eccentricities."

After we had ordered our meals Irene presented us with tickets for her concert, which was scheduled for Wednesday evening. She gave us a brief summary of the plot of *Madama Butterfly*, which struck me as controversial — both in terms of its inter-racial and extramarital themes and its violent ending. I was glad that we would be attending a concert version of Puccini's opera, so we would only be introduced to the music, which Irene assured us was exceptional.

We were able to get through the entire evening without any discussion of the events that had taken place in Saint Louis. The press had reported the explosion of a dirigible at the fair, but since there had not been mass casualties the incident had not generated a great deal of attention, and both Golding and Rhymes had done a good job of suppressing all information about the fourteen individuals who had been infected with the virus.

At the end of our dinner I was not surprised when Godfrey demanded that we permit him to pay the bill. "I would not be here this evening if it was not for you gentlemen. Irene and I will be forever in your debt." He also informed us that he had been made a full partner at his law firm. We congratulated him on this very good news, which served as a happy culmination of a much-needed evening of good company and good food.

Thirty

Abrams arrived at the Algonquin while we were finishing our breakfast the next morning. He presented Holmes with a sheet of paper. "Seven names, with basic financial and biographical information for each one. I think that you will be particularly interested in the third person on the list. I gather that he is — was — especially friendly with General Smythe. I was also able to confirm that Smythe recently invested a large portion of his personal savings in this man's company."

Holmes scanned the list and then stated that he agreed that this person should be given priority.

Abrams could not resist the temptation. "Yes, it does seem elementary to me." I rewarded him with a smile, but Holmes simply went on reading with no change of expression. When he had finished reading the list he gave it to me and I could see immediately why Abrams had identified this person as a suspect. He spoke as I read the information: "Brian Henson is the president of Henson Pharmaceuticals. It is a medium size company that produces some widely used drugs. It also has a small laboratory — about thirty scientists — who are involved in original research. For the last six years they have focused on the quest for vaccines for certain types of viruses."

"Excellent police work, Inspector Abrams," Holmes stated. "I think that this information justifies obtaining a search warrant for Henson Pharmaceuticals, so that we will have it at hand in case we need to move quickly — before Henson can destroy any evidence that might implicate him in the Saint Louis crimes."

"As for the warrant, I can attempt to convince a judge, but I may meet with some resistance there."

Holmes reassured Abrams, "I think I can be of some assistance in that regard, if you can give me the name of the judge." Abrams provided the name and Holmes began to stand up. "Now, if you will excuse us, Watson and I have an appointment at the Anglo-Saxon Club at one this afternoon. We will use this opportunity to gain some information about the Club in general, and about Dr Henson in particular. Let us plan to meet back here at the hotel at four, to discuss next steps." Abrams departed and Holmes went to the reception desk to use the telephone.

My friend and I returned to our rooms for an hour and then departed for the Anglo-Saxon Club. We engaged a carriage and arrived at our destination a bit early, and somewhat chilled. Since the club was close to the Waldorf Hotel, we decided to go inside to warm up. The hotel had a well-deserved reputation for opulence. The high-ceilinged lobby was impressive, with numerous works of art and ornate cabinetry imported from Europe. We were directed to the billiard room which served as a café in the daytime. We both ordered coffee, and used the time to discuss our strategy for the visit to the Anglo-Saxon Club. We left the hotel impressed and invigorated.

We were greeted at the entrance to the Anglo-Saxon Club by a Mr Baldwin, who informed us that he had agreed to serve as acting president of the club now that 'the general' had passed away. "It is a great tragedy. The general is irreplaceable. I hope that you gentlemen will be able to provide us with some information on the circumstances of his death."

Holmes and I removed our overcoats and my friend thanked our host for meeting with us on short notice. "We had limited contact with General Smythe in Saint Louis, but we felt the need to meet with his friends in the Anglo-Saxon Club to offer our condolences."

Baldwin ushered us into the main room of the club, where a small group of well-dressed gentlemen were socializing. As planned, we split up and began to work our way through the group, shaking hands and expressing our sympathies. We encouraged the members to discuss the goals and activities of the club, even though we had heard some of this information from Smythe during the reception at the White House.

When I finally reconnected with Holmes he was speaking with a blond-haired man with a trim moustache who appeared to be in his early forties. Holmes introduced him to me as Dr Henson.

"It is a pleasure to meet a fellow physician, Dr Watson. I regret that you are here under these unfortunate circumstances."

"Unfortunate indeed, Dr Henson. I had only a brief interaction with General Smythe, but he impressed me as a natural leader of men. Please accept our sincere condolences at his loss."

"The general was a close friend. We shared an interest in the history of British-American relations and a commitment to the values associated with the Anglo-Saxon creed; individual liberty, laissez faire economics, democracy, the social contract. This club is dedicated to the perpetuation of those values. General Smythe will be sorely missed."

I paused for a few moments and then inquired about Henson's field of expertise.

"I am an immunologist. I studied medicine at Harvard University and then spent two years working at the Pasteur Institute in Paris. I am now the head of a small pharmaceutical company which is located in Brooklyn."

I was about to launch into some comments on the impressive work of the Pasteur Institute when Holmes intervened. "I assume that you have seen some of the speculation by the press to the effect that General Smythe was involved in some form of criminal activity in Saint Louis."

"I have, but I reject these scurrilous rumours out of hand. I know the man, and he is not the kind of person to engage in the kidnapping and murder of a bunch of Asians."

Holmes apologised immediately. "We did not come here to cast aspersions. I am sure that you are correct about the general's character, and that these accusations will be proven false."

We continued to exchange pleasantries with the members of the club for another hour and then were able to depart. By the time we exited the building the temperature had dropped even further, and a light snow was falling. Holmes flagged down a hansom cab and instructed the driver to make all haste to our hotel. He offered him a generous inducement for his efforts. Once we were settled in, Holmes rubbed his hands together. He was clearly excited. "Watson, we cannot afford to waste time. I hope that our man Abrams will be waiting for us, and ready to take action, when we get to the hotel."

It was not clear to me what had transpired at the Anglo-Saxon Club that had made my friend so excited, but I knew Holmes, and I knew that he was close to closing the trap.

Holmes nearly jumped down from the Hansom when we arrived. I followed him into the lobby of the Algonquin and was pleased to see Abrams, with four armed police officers.

Holmes shook his hand. "I am glad to see you, Inspector. I can report that we have confirmed our suspicions about Dr Henson and we can now move quickly to confront him at his laboratory in Brooklyn. I assume that you had no trouble acquiring the search and arrest warrants?"

Abrams laughed. "The judge has already framed the telegram from President Roosevelt in support of my request. I suspect that I will be able to obtain warrants from him whenever I need them for the rest of my career."

"Splendid." At that moment the concierge interrupted Holmes and presented him with a note. He scanned it and then returned to our group and stated, "We should only have to wait for a few more minutes before departing."

I was about to ask Holmes what we were waiting for, when my question was answered. Theodore Roosevelt came storming into the lobby along with Joseph Walks Far and two other individuals who were apparently members of the Secret Service. Joseph was carrying a large envelope.

The president shook our hands and then said, "Greetings, Sherlock. I assume you got my telegram informing you of my desire to join the party." Holmes nodded and indicated the folded note in his hand. "As soon as I got your telephone message this morning I cancelled all of my obligations for the day and headed here with my 'rough riders' — he gestured toward his bodyguards. "It helps when you are the president and can commandeer a train at short notice."

"Your trip is not in vain, Mr President. Watson and I have now confirmed the identity of the main culprit in this plot. His name is Dr Brian Henson. We spoke with him a short time ago, and he inadvertently confirmed his guilt."

I was surprised by this comment. "How did he slip up, Holmes?"

"You will remember, Watson, that when we visited the Anglo-Saxon Club I mentioned to Dr Henson that there had been some very unpleasant rumours about General Smythe's activities in Saint Louis. Henson responded that the general was not the kind of man who would kidnap and murder a group of Asians. As you know, Mr Golding, the chief of the Saint Louis Police, did inform the press that Smythe was under investigation for kidnapping, but on my advice neither he nor any of his subordinates mentioned that the victims were Asians. This information could only be available to Henson because he was a party to the crime. I think that we should now move expeditiously to confront Dr Henson in his lair."

Thirty-One

Abrams made a call and within minutes our group was on our way to Brooklyn in three large police wagons. We travelled downtown and then across the Brooklyn Bridge, and ten minutes later we arrived at our destination. Abrams and Joseph had travelled together, along with the president and me. They used the time to discuss their respective duties. It was agreed that the New York Police would take responsibility for exercising the warrants and searching the building. The Secret Service agents would remain with the president to insure his safety and serve as a backup for the New York officers if they were needed.

We entered a small building — four stories, with the top two floors serving as laboratories. We were met in the lobby by a young woman who gasped when she saw the president and our heavily armed entourage. "Welcome to Henson Pharmaceuticals, gentlemen... Mr Roosevelt... How can I be of service?"

Abrams took the lead. "We would like to speak with Dr Henson. Is he available?"

"He is in a meeting at present, in our second-floor conference room." The receptionist pointed to the stairs. Abrams thanked her and our group moved quickly up to the second floor. We saw Henson in a glassed-in room, standing at the head of a long table and speaking to a small group of men whom we assumed to be his employees. Abrams knocked on the door and then immediately opened it. His intention was to make it clear to everyone in the room that he was in charge, but all eyes were focused on the president. "Dr Henson, I presume. I am Detective Inspector Abrams of the New York City Police Department." He did not introduce anyone else in our group. "We would like to speak with you in private." He looked around the room and then said, "Immediately." Everyone seated at the table scrambled to vacate the room. When they were gone, Henson sat down at the head of the table and attempted to gain control of the situation. "I hope that you have some very good reason for interrupting an important meeting, gentlemen."

Abrams drew two documents out of his breast pocket. "These warrants, for your arrest and for a comprehensive search of these premises, constitute a very good reason."

Henson was clearly a strong personality, who was not cowed by Abrams. "And what, exactly, am I accused of?"

"The warrant for your arrest accuses you of conspiring with General Smythe to release a deadly plague at the Saint Louis World's Fair, an action that would have jeopardised the lives of thousands of people."

"But this is madness. I am a doctor, and like Dr Watson, I have taken an oath to do no harm. What possible motive would I have for spreading a plague? And for that matter, what possible reason would General Smythe have for joining me in this outrageous crime?"

Holmes responded, "As to your motives, Dr Henson, the answer is simple... money. I am confident that when we inspect your laboratories today we will find not only samples of the virus which will match the samples that have been collected in Saint Louis, but also samples of a vaccine for this particular form of the plague. It does not take a leap of imagination to conclude that you were planning to work with Smythe to spread the virus and then, once it began to spread across the United States and public hysteria began to take root, you would declare the good news that your exceptional team of scientists had discovered a vaccine which could be mass produced very quickly, with sufficient funding from the federal government. You would walk away from this crime not only enormously wealthy, but also celebrated as a national hero."

"I am prepared to concede that my laboratories have been working on the development of a vaccine for a particular form of Bacterium Pestis, and that in order to develop this vaccine we have stockpiled a quantity of the live virus. But I can only conclude that if the virus has been discovered in Saint Louis, then it must have been stolen from our laboratory. As for my so-called conspiracy with General Smythe, I suppose it is possible that he was the person responsible for stealing the virus in the service of some nefarious plot. But I cannot, for the life of me, imagine what motive he would have for doing such a thing."

Holmes responded at this point. "It is at least conceivable that the vaccine and the virus could have been stolen from your laboratory without your knowledge. I also admit that I can think of no good reason why General Smythe would attempt the indiscriminate distribution of a deadly virus."

My friend's comments seemed to encourage Henson. But he was immediately deflated by Holmes' next words. "If this was the state's entire case it might make sense for you to gamble on a jury trial, Dr Henson. But our case against you goes much further."

Roosevelt took charge of the discussion at this point. "It has come to our attention that you have been engaged not only in a plot against the American people but also a plot against me, personally."

"Now you are speaking complete nonsense. What evidence could you possibly have to support this accusation?"

Joseph handed the president the large envelope that he had been carrying. Mr Roosevelt removed two pieces of paper and handed the first one to Henson. We had all read the document, so we knew its contents. It was very brief:

Leonid, we failed in our first effort to kill TR, but we cannot afford to fail a second time. Let's meet to discuss next steps.
3 1 5 / 40

The letter was typed on good quality stationery, and signed Brian.

Holmes picked up the argument at this point. "As you may know, Dr Henson, typewriters often exhibit distinctive flaws, which make them almost as good as finger-marks as a form of identification. The typewriter that was used for this brief message has a defective small E. Our agents have a warrant to search your office and your home, and we will certainly inspect any typewriters that we find. We will also be looking for samples of stationery that match the note that you signed. We will, of course, also call upon experts to ascertain the authenticity of your signature."

Henson began to speak, but was interrupted by Roosevelt. "Then there is this…" The president handed Henson a photograph. "The numbers in your brief message to the Russian Ambassador were clearly a code, designed to inform Mr Ivanov of the time, date, and location of the proposed meeting — three p.m., one day from now, 5th Avenue and 40th Street. It was simple enough, but we were still trying to break the code yesterday when you met with the ambassador at the southeast corner of Bryant Park. Fortunately, we did not need to solve the code since we have had the Russian Ambassador under close surveillance for some time now. So we were following him when he left his embassy and met you in the park."

Henson stared at the photo of himself speaking with someone. "I have never met the Russian Ambassador. And

I did not have a meeting with this person." He looked back at the photo and then stated, "I remember now. This individual stopped me when I was walking to lunch yesterday. He asked me for a match and I said that I do not smoke and could not help him. He thanked me and walked away. The entire exchange could not have lasted more than a minute."

Roosevelt kept up the offensive. "So that is going to be your defence in court?" He waved the photo. "You should understand that not only does this constitute very convincing evidence, but it also elevates the crime to treason — collaborating with a foreign government in an attempt to kill an American president. Treason is a unique crime that is actually adjudicated by Congress. The punishment is either death or imprisonment for not less than five years. Being good politicians, the members of Congress will recognise that there is no advantage in favouring leniency and everything to be gained by appearing bloodthirsty. I would not be surprised if both houses voted unanimously for an expeditious death sentence. The law does not stipulate the method of execution, but I would assume that it will be the same that was used for the murderer of President McKinley — he was electrocuted, requiring three jolts to kill him."

Henson's face was a bright red, and I began to think that he was in danger of a stroke. "This is a complete fabrication," he shouted. "The note is a forgery, and the photo is clearly staged to send a misleading message."

Roosevelt responded that he was confident that the signature on the message could be validated. "And before you think about engaging counsel and preparing your defence, you should know that when we confronted the ambassador with this evidence he reminded us that he has full diplomatic immunity, but when we threatened to designate him persona non grata and send him back to Russia he relented and offered to assist the government in its case against you, as long as his name was kept out of it. If this was a normal criminal case rather than a matter for congress we could not have agreed to his terms, but treason is an entirely different matter."

Then the president stated, "But there is still a way out for you. For diplomatic reasons it would be best if the entire treason case could be avoided. We have our own ways of punishing Moscow, which are best kept confidential. This gives you an opportunity. If you elect to plead guilty to conspiracy in the killing of the fourteen Asians and in the attempt to release the airborne pathogen, if you provide us with a thorough explanation of your motives and actions and include information on all of your accomplices, you will be prosecuted in Saint Louis. You will probably receive a sentence of twenty-five years, with no possibility of parole. For its part, the government will not move forward with the charge of treason. This is a one-time offer."

I remember thinking at the time that this sounded like very mild punishment for a person who had contrived to jeopardise the lives of thousands of people. But then I reminded myself that much of our case against Henson was concocted, and we had assured the Russian Ambassador that his involvement in this case would be limited to the photograph. The president's comments notwithstanding, Ivanov had made it clear that he would not testify in court or assist the prosecution in any other way. Under these circumstances, I concluded that, once again, we needed to settle for half a loaf.

Before leaving with our prisoner we instructed him to take us to his laboratory. He led us upstairs and showed us the vials of both the virus and the vaccine. I was glad to see that they were stored in a secure section of the laboratory. Abrams left two of his officers in the laboratory with instructions to allow no one in. Then he contacted his precinct and arranged for around the clock protection of the facility.

As it turned out, Henson was the only person in the laboratory involved in the plot to spread the plague. Once this was confirmed we were able to rely upon the other researchers in the company to assist in the dismantlement of the laboratory and the safe relocation of the virus and vaccine.

Thirty-Two

The following is my statement regarding the circumstances surrounding my cooperation with General Allen Smythe in a plot to kill fourteen individuals and release a dangerous pathogen at the Saint Louis World's Fair. I make this statement of my own free will, in accordance with my plea of guilty to the above crimes.

I can trace my involvement in this plot to a conversation that I had with General Smythe at the Anglo-Saxon Club one year ago. I was very excited to inform my friend that my pharmaceutical company had made great progress in our efforts to develop a vaccine for a particular strain of pneumonic plague. I said that although this version of the plague was not active in the United States the announcement of this discovery would still insure a dramatic increase in the price of my company's stock. I encouraged Smythe to take advantage of this information to invest in the company before we made a public announcement.

The next day Smythe visited me in my office. The general said that he knew that I shared his deep concern that the indispensable Anglo-American relationship was in jeopardy under President Roosevelt. "The future hinges on

Roosevelt's success at controlling the Philippines. Once he has achieved this goal he will be able to use Manila as a jumping off point for regional dominance, at the expense of the transatlantic relationship. This will be a major setback for Great Britain, but it will be an even greater disaster for America. The open door will inevitably swing both ways, and the United States will be flooded with Asians — who cannot possibly share, or even comprehend, our foundational values."

The general continued. "The situation is now at a tipping point. Domestic opposition to Roosevelt's Asian adventurism is already widespread, but not sufficiently intense to overcome the president's influence. But imagine the hostility to the president's plan if a horrific plague could be traced directly to the Filipino natives and the other Asians currently residing at the Saint Louis World's Fair."

I agreed to assist General Smythe by providing him with a sufficient quantity of the virus to kill the captive Asians and to spread the pathogen by means of his airship over a large area of the World's Fair. To cover the theft and to avoid interference by any of my researchers I informed them that I had discovered some anomalies in our vaccine and I would be working by myself to address these problems. They were also given strict instructions not to discuss our research with anyone outside of the laboratory, on the grounds that it would seriously harm the market value of the vaccine.

During his time in Saint Louis, General Smythe recruited a few individuals to assist him with his plans to kidnap and kill Asians and to maintain his dirigible. I had no involvement with these persons and do not know their identities.

In conclusion, I sincerely regret my involvement in this affair, and I ask the court to take into consideration my long career as a physician and my contributions to medical knowledge as a researcher.

Thirty-Three

After breakfast at the Algonquin I spent the rest of the day preparing for the evening's concert. On the advice of our concierge I took a carriage to 'book row' on 4th Avenue, where I was able to find an English translation of the libretto for Puccini's *Madama Butterfly*. I also obtained a copy of John Luther Long's short story by the same title. I returned to the Algonquin, where I settled in to consume both publications. They were not light reading. The two versions of the tragic life and death of the main character were almost enough to convince me to beg off of the evening's concert. But the prospect of hearing Mrs Norton perform was irresistible.

Holmes and I walked from our hotel to the Metropolitan Opera on Broadway and 39th Street. We met Godfrey Norton at the entrance and he guided us to our seats in the front orchestra section of the opera house. The concert hall was full that evening, and it was clear from the applause when Mrs Norton walked onto the stage that the audience was full of her enthusiastic fans. Because it was a concert format rather than a staged opera, the performers were dressed in formal wear rather than costumes. Irene wore a stunning green gown, which was accented by a single emerald mounted on a gold necklace.

Every aspect of the performance was memorable. Irene received multiple standing ovations for her arias. Her rendition of the song titled *un bel di* was particularly beautiful and evocative. The man who sang the role of Pinkerton, the American naval officer, impressed us with his clear, strong tenor voice. The orchestra and chorus were excellent, particularly in their rendition of what our programs described as the 'humming chorus'.

When we met Irene backstage at the conclusion of the concert she introduced us to "my Pinkerton." The young tenor, whose name was Enrico Caruso, greeted us enthusiastically. He lavished praise on Irene, describing her as "a prima donna of incomparable talent and beauty." He produced a gold case and offered each of us one of his dark brown cigarettes before lighting one for himself.

Holmes accepted his offer, but did not light it. He ran the unlit cigarette under his nose, as I had seen him do many times, and stated, "An interesting brand. Egyptian, very strong, similar to the shag that I rely upon from time to time to assist me in thinking through a particularly complex problem. With your permission, Mr Caruso, I will add this to my collection of tobacco types."

"By all means, Mr Holmes. I hope you will permit me to claim that I have helped in some small way to enrich the knowledge of the world's greatest consulting detective."

After Irene changed into casual clothing our group, which now included Caruso, used the performers exit and walked back to the bar at the Algonquin. When we were settled in and had ordered cocktails Godfrey pressed us to report on our adventures in Saint Louis.

I began by stating that "anything that we tell you will have to go no further than this table." They assured me that they would hold our discussion in strictest confidence. I began by describing the fair, and then explained our collaboration with Rhymes, Golding and Loving, and our disruption of the attempt on the president's life.

When I began to describe Holmes' pursuit of the assassin my friend interrupted me. "Watson, please resist the temptation to exaggerate and romanticise your account." To placate my friend I gave only a brief summary of the chase through The Hereafter and simply stated that the criminal met his death in an accident while attempting to escape. I decided not to report on our discovery of the victims in the warehouse and the shed, and jumped right to our dramatic confrontation with General Smythe and the Victoria.

"When Holmes jumped from the Great Wheel I thought that he had surely missed his target. I have not been that shocked since we confronted that hellish hound on the moors of Devon." I skimmed over the conclusion to this part of the story, since I knew that Holmes would be discomfited if I gave the dramatic conclusion the detailed account that it deserved. I then moved quickly through our return to New York, our discovery of Smythe's conspirator at the Anglo-Saxon Club, and our cooperation with the

New York Police Department to arrest Dr Henson at his place of business.

"It is an amazing story, Dr Watson," Godfrey said, "but I fail to understand why anyone would want to release a plague on the United States unless they were completely mad."

Holmes responded, "We asked ourselves that same question, Godfrey, and we finally received an answer yesterday, when Dr Henson provided us with a thorough statement at the time of his arrest. The use of the plague was General Smythe's idea. His goal was to implicate Asians in general and Filipinos in particular in the spread of the plague across the nation. He believed that if Asians could be blamed for bringing the plague to America it would convince the public to turn away from that region and return to a foreign policy that prioritises Europe in general and Great Britain in particular."

"And Henson?"

Holmes said, "I see him as an even greater villain than Smythe, since his actions were primarily guided by a quest for wealth and personal prestige. Also, he was answerable to the Hippocratic Oath, which imposed additional ethical responsibilities on him. By comparison, Smythe was simply delusional. This certainly does not exonerate him, but it does help to explain why he was willing to cause a large number of deaths in the service of his grand plan."

When our group fell silent Irene signalled the waiter for another round of cocktails. "I think it is time to shift to a less depressing topic of conversation, Sherlock, and I think that Godfrey can cheer us up with some interesting news."

"Thank you, my dear. I assume that the news to which my wife refers is that I have been asked by my partners to open a branch of our firm in San Francisco. If I accept this invitation we will have to postpone the move to California until Irene completes her upcoming European tour. The partners are perfectly willing to wait. Irene and I have been discussing this, and we should be able to give my firm an answer by next week."

I congratulated Godfrey and said, "This sounds like a very exciting opportunity. May I ask, Irene, how this move will affect your career at a time when you are enjoying an international reputation?"

"Thank you for asking, Doctor. It will certainly pose some challenges for me. But I am encouraged by friends and colleagues based in California who have assured me that San Francisco is a dynamic and wealthy city that is on the verge of establishing itself as a centre for classical music in general and opera in particular. I admit that I am attracted to the idea of being involved in this type of enterprise."

After we finished our cocktails, Holmes and I escorted our guests out of the hotel. We were saying goodbye to our friends when we were confronted by a man in a heavy black coat, a large-brimmed hat and a black scarf. His head was down until he was in front of us.

"Well, Smythe, you make a very dramatic entrance. Have you come to give yourself up?"

The man tilted his head up. "No, Holmes. I have come to give you the reward that you deserve for your betrayal of both your country and mine." With that, Smythe twisted the head of his cane and pulled out a long-bladed knife. Holmes and I both removed revolvers from our pockets. "As you can see, we have been expecting you. Tonight was the first time I have taken a gun to an opera performance, which is probably fortunate for some of the execrable tenors that I have heard in the past. I would advise you to put down your knife. As a military man I am sure you recognise when surrender is the only option."

Smythe moved surprisingly quickly. He grabbed Irene and put the knife to her throat. "As a military man, I recognise that sometimes it is necessary to change the balance of power. Now, gentlemen, put down your weapons or I will kill this lady."

Suddenly, Irene gave a loud sigh and collapsed to the pavement. Both Holmes and I fired without hesitation, and Smythe collapsed at our feet. I immediately went to Irene, fearing that she had been stabbed. I knelt beside her and she placed her hand on mine. "Don't be concerned, Doctor, I have been fainting as a career for two decades, although I must say, this was a particularly effective performance." Norton bent down and helped his wife to stand.

While we waited for the police Holmes spoke to Irene. "I do apologise for putting you in danger. Watson and I did not expect Smythe to attack us in this way. We actually assumed that he was probably already out of the country.

But we took the necessary precautions with our pistols, in case we were wrong."

Norton responded on behalf of his wife. "But Holmes, you cannot be blamed. We were all under the impression that Smythe had perished at the World's Fair."

"We believed the same thing at first, Godfrey. But just to be sure, I sent a telegram to the doctor in Saint Louis who had assisted us in our investigation. I asked him to confirm that the person who had been killed in the dirigible had a wooden leg. In spite of the fact that the body was severely damaged the doctor was able to assure us that the dead man did not have a prosthesis. We reported this to the New York and Saint Louis Police Departments, who have been engaged in their own investigations, but we also decided to be prepared for any eventuality."

Our group returned to the lobby of the hotel, where Holmes telephoned Detective Abrams and reported on what had transpired. When Abrams arrived he asked for our accounts of what had happened. After about an hour he thanked us and informed us that we could now leave. We said our goodbyes. Caruso laughed and said, "Congratulations, Mr Holmes and Doctor Watson, and thank you for providing me with a truly operatic story. Then he kissed Irene's hand and stated that he was looking forward to their next collaboration. "Scala, I believe."

The Nortons also rose to leave, after thanking us once again for our help and promising to keep us informed of Irene's European concert schedule. "I will be sure to add a few performances in London so that we can have a reunion."

After the police left, Holmes and I agreed that we deserved another brandy. "I am looking forward to getting back to Baker Street, Watson. Hasting's has already made arrangements for a return trip on the *Lucania*."

"About that, Holmes. I am afraid that you will have to travel back to England by yourself. I intend to return to Saint Louis for another week of tourism. I will ask Hastings to cancel my reservation."

"That won't be necessary, Watson. When I said that Hastings has already made arrangements I was referring only to myself. I advised him that I would be returning alone and that you would be following at a later date."

"But how could you know about my change of plans, Holmes?"

"My good friend, after all these years I can read you like a book, especially on issues relating to the fairer sex. Have you already informed Miss Zamora of your plans?"

I was about to protest, but then I simply smiled and said, "Yes, I have been in touch with the lady and she has graciously agreed to carve out some time for me during my visit."

My friend laughed at my carefully worded reply, which triggered a laugh on my part as well.

Thirty-Four

I returned to Baker Street in early January. Soon after my arrival we were summoned by Mycroft. We met him, once again, in the Stranger's Room at the Diogenes Club.

Holmes began the conversation with his brother. "We were fortunate that you decided not to leave New York until Dr Henson was exposed and arrested. We were also lucky that you were able to call upon some of your resources on very short notice. By my count, you were assisted by at least three individuals: One to steal the stationery from Henson's office and type the note to the ambassador on Henson's machine, one to forge Henson's signature on the note, and one to take the photograph of Henson's brief meeting with the ambassador in Gramercy Park. And of course, the whole thing depended on the ambassador's participation."

Mycroft nodded. "Indeed. As you know, Ivanov was in my debt, because I had kept silent about his role in the two attempts on the president's life, and because I had allowed him to construct whatever story he liked in his report to his superiors in Moscow. I had also assured him that the photo of his meeting with Henson would be destroyed after it had served its purpose. Fortunately,

Henson did not test our claim that the ambassador was prepared to testify against him. My only regret is that I had to call in my debt from the Russian ambassador so soon after acquiring that bit of leverage."

Our host said, "I do have one final question, Sherlock: If Smythe was not in the cabin of the *Victoria*, then who was?"

"The Saint Louis police are still looking into it, but I suspect that we will never know. The general was assisted at the fair by at least six men, and any one of them, or some other person, could have been the pilot of the airship. Nor will we ever know if Smythe's decision to allow someone else to pilot the dirigible was a last-minute change of plans or something that had been scheduled in advance."

After some minutes of silence, Holmes observed that "this has been a unique case, in that we were dealing with two tracks — the Russian-sponsored attacks on the American president and the more ambitious plot by Henson and Smythe to spread the plague. And in the end we were able to use references to the first track to convince Henson to plead guilty to the second."

Mycroft added, "It is also ironic that, in the grand scheme of things, Britain would probably have been better served if Smythe had succeeded in terrorizing America and convincing Washington to return to a Europe-first foreign policy. Because of its special relationship with the United States, London would once again have been the principal beneficiary of this reorientation."

With that last controversial observation, Mycroft bid us farewell. He chose not to rise to shake our hands, for fear, I am sure, that he would be sanctioned by other club members for being disruptive.

Conclusion

I spent the first half of 1905 completing my account of Holmes' and my adventure in the United States. Before I could complete it, however, I was advised by representatives of both the American and British governments that I could not publish it. I was frustrated, of course, but I nonetheless understood why the two governments demanded that I exercise self-censorship. The international atmosphere at the start of the twentieth century has turned extremely tense, and I would not want to contribute to the mood of suspicion and acrimony by releasing some of the details of this case. I leave it to those individuals who will open this document in the twenty first century to decide if it is safe by then to publish this account. Prudens Futuri.